Hi, I'm **JIMMY!**

Like me, you probably noticed the world is run by adults.
But ask yourself: Who would do the best job
of making books that *kids* will love?
Yeah. **Kids!**

So that's how the idea of **JIMMY** books came to life.
We want every **JIMMY** book to be so good that when you're finished,
you'll say,
"PLEASE GIVE ME ANOTHER BOOK!"

Give this one a try and see if you agree.
(If not, you're probably an adult!)

JIMMY PATTERSON BOOKS FOR YOUNG READERS

James Patterson Presents

Sci-Fi Junior High by John Martin and Scott Seegert
Sci-Fi Junior High: Crash Landing by John Martin and Scott Seegert
How to Be a Supervillain by Michael Fry

The Middle School Series by James Patterson

Middle School: The Worst Years of My Life
Middle School: Get Me Out of Here!
Middle School: Big Fat Liar
Middle School: How I Survived Bullies, Broccoli, and Snake Hill
Middle School: Ultimate Showdown
Middle School: Save Rafe!
Middle School: Just My Rotten Luck
Middle School: Dog's Best Friend
Middle School: Escape to Australia

The I Funny Series by James Patterson

I Funny
I Even Funnier
I Totally Funniest
I Funny TV
I Funny: School of Laughs

The Treasure Hunters Series by James Patterson

Treasure Hunters
Treasure Hunters: Danger Down the Nile
Treasure Hunters: Secret of the Forbidden City
Treasure Hunters: Peril at the Top of the World
Treasure Hunters: A Quest for the City of Gold

The House of Robots Series by James Patterson

House of Robots
House of Robots: Robots Go Wild!
House of Robots: Robot Revolution

The Daniel X Series by James Patterson

The Dangerous Days of Daniel X
Daniel X: Watch the Skies
Daniel X: Demons and Druids
Daniel X: Game Over
Daniel X: Armageddon
Daniel X: Lights Out

Other Illustrated Novels and Stories

Jacky Ha-Ha
Jacky Ha-Ha: My Life Is a Joke
Laugh Out Loud
Pottymouth and Stoopid
Word of Mouse
Public School Superhero
Give Please a Chance
Give Thank You a Try
Big Words for Little Geniuses

For exclusives, trailers, and other information, visit jimmypatterson.org.

JACKY HA-HA

MY LIFE IS A JOKE

JAMES PATTERSON

AND **CHRIS GRABENSTEIN**

ILLUSTRATED BY **KERASCOËT**

JIMMY Patterson Books
LITTLE, BROWN AND COMPANY
NEW YORK BOSTON LONDON

JIMMY Patterson Books / Little, Brown and Company
Hachette Book Group
1290 Avenue of the Americas, New York, NY 10104
JIMMYPatterson.org

First Edition: October 2017

JIMMY Patterson Books is an imprint of Little, Brown and Company, a division of Hachette Book Group, Inc. The Little, Brown name and logo are trademarks of Hachette Book Group, Inc. The JIMMY Patterson Books® name and logo are trademarks of JBP Business, LLC.

Library of Congress Cataloging-in-Publication Data

Names: Patterson, James, author. | Grabenstein, Chris, author. | Kerascoët, illustrator.
Title: Jacky Ha-Ha : my life is a joke / James Patterson, Chris Grabenstein ; illustrated by Kerascoët.
Description: First edition. | New York ; Boston : Jimmy Patterson Books/Little, Brown and Company, 2017. | Series: Jacky Ha-Ha ; 2 | Summary: "Jacky Hart has found a hidden talent in the performing arts, and she's a triple threat onstage! She wants nothing more than to act and sing all summer—but her parents have other plans for her"—Provided by publisher.
Identifiers: LCCN 2017009627 | ISBN 9780316433761 (hardcover)
Subjects: | CYAC: Summer employment—Fiction. | Theater—Fiction. | Stuttering—Fiction. | Family life—New Jersey—Fiction. | New Jersey—History—20th century—Fiction. | Humorous stories. | BISAC: JUVENILE FICTION / Humorous Stories. | JUVENILE FICTION / Performing Arts / Theater. | JUVENILE FICTION / Girls & Women. | JUVENILE FICTION / Family / Parents. | JUVENILE FICTION / Family / Siblings. | JUVENILE FICTION / Historical / United States / 20th Century. | JUVENILE FICTION / Performing Arts / General.
Classification: LCC PZ7.P27653 Jaf 2017 | DDC [Fic]—dc23
LC record available at https://lccn.loc.gov/2017009627

10 9 8 7 6 5 4 3 2 1

LSC-H

Printed in the United States of America

For the Knoxville Children's Theatre
—C. G.

PROLOGUE

Greetings from jolly old England, darling daughters, where I am feeling anything but jolly.

In fact, I might be having a panic attack.

My heart is racing. My palms feel clammy, which is a strange expression, because how can hands feel like clams?

Anyway, I can barely breathe and it's not because somebody just told me what the cute-sounding British dish "bubble and squeak" actually is (leftover vegetables mashed together with cabbage, potatoes, and anything else nobody wanted to eat the day before).

I haven't been this nervous since the time I climbed the Ferris wheel down the shore in Seaside Heights, New Jersey. (The second time. The time my dad caught me.)

I think I am freaking out because I am about to do something I've always wanted to do but am totally terrified of doing.

Yes, that makes about as much sense as a book titled *How to Read* or a waterproof towel.

As you ladies know, your famous mom is over here in London, rehearsing for William Shakespeare's play *As You Like It* at the Globe Theatre.

This is called Tudor architecture, even though it has more than two doors!

I'm playing Rosalind, one of Shakespeare's funniest, most kick-butt female characters. The new Globe is a re-creation of his famous theater from back in 1599, which, believe it or not, was a year or two before I was born.

Life is good, right?

No. Life right now is *terrifying!*

Sh-Sh-Shakespeare.

Just thinking about playing a part in a comedy by the *Greatest Writer Who Ever Lived* with one of the finest Shakespearean acting companies in the world (or, you know, the *globe*) makes me extremely shaky.

So why is my big opportunity such a huge nightmare?

Because it reminds me of one of the most colossal failures in my whole, entire life.

Most people may know me as the super-cool Academy Award–winning funny lady and star of *Saturday Night Live,* but that's not who I was one summer when I was about your age.

I was a mess.

And a failure.

The star of a one-woman disaster movie.

Yes, girls, you guessed it. There's an embarrassingly kooky but meaningful story from my younger days in your immediate future.

So beware: There are hazardous conditions up ahead.

CHAPTER 1

It's the summer of 1991.

Teenage Mutant Ninja Turtles toys are huge. So is Rollerblade Barbie. What are Rollerblades? Don't worry, you don't need to know. Unless you want to twist your ankle, sprain your butt, and scrape most of the skin off your elbows like I did.

Someday, I'll probably look back on this and LAUGH.
Today, I think I'll just SCREAM in AGONY.

Everybody is saying "*Hasta la vista,* baby" to each other, and not just in Spanish class, because Ah-nold Schwarzenegger said it in a movie called *Terminator 2: Judgment Day.*

In fact, 1991 started out pretty good, especially if you ignored Boyz II Men on the radio. (Yep, they were a thing. And that *II?* It's supposed to be a Roman numeral two, not an eleven.)

In March, Mom came home from Operation Desert Shield, which turned into Operation Desert Storm—a war that, thankfully, only lasted, like, six weeks. Now she's back in charge of running the Hart house.

Did I mention my mom, Big Sydney Hart, was a marine? (She's Big because my sister Little Sydney is named after her.)

"I want to see those dishes shine, girls!" she tells us every night after dinner. "I want this galley to glisten!"

"Aye, aye!" we all say.

"Hoo-ah!" says Mom.

Emma, the youngest, who we used to call the Little Boss, is now the Little Echo. She tells us to do whatever Mom just told us to do.

PUT SOME ELBOW GREASE INTO IT, GIRLS!
PUT SOME GREASE ON YOUR ELBOWS, GIRLS!

Things are humming along at school, too.

Yours truly hasn't had a detention since I played Snoopy in the fall musical, *You're a Good Man, Charlie Brown.* If you knew me at all, you knew that me not having detention was a miracle!

I also did the spring show—*You Can't Take It with You.* It was a comedy (yay!) and I played Essie Carmichael, a kooky candymaker who dreams of being a ballerina even though she's a terrible dancer.

I was hysterical, girls. Your mother always was (and always will be) a terrible dancer. Terrible can be funny. Especially if it's ballet.

So now it's June, and life is pretty sweet. Mom's home safe and sound. School's almost over. I'm looking forward to a fun-in-the-sun Jersey Shore summer. The beach! The boardwalk! Bill Phillips!

Yes, he still has those crazy-gorgeous hazel eyes and I still have a kind-of, sort-of crush on him. Hey, I'm twelve going on thirteen. It's summer. It happens.

My big plans when school's out?

Goofing off. Lazing around. Hitting the beach. Doing a whole lot of *nothing.*

Unfortunately, Dad and Mom have different plans.

Very different.

CHAPTER 2

"Girls?" says Mom when the dishes are cleaned, dried, and put away and she's all out of *hoo-ah*s. "Your father will be home in fifteen minutes."

"Should we have saved some chicken pot pie for him?" asks Hannah. She's fourteen and super-sweet. "I would've skipped my second helping if I knew Dad was coming home in time to eat. . . ."

"What about the third helping?" asks Sophia. She's eighteen and the second oldest or, as she likes to put it, the "oldest sister still living at home," because Little Sydney, who's nineteen, is in college at Princeton. Hannah and Sophia are both kind of boy-crazy. And sometimes, they're both crazy about the same boy at the same time.

Awk-ward.

"If you want my opinion," says Victoria, who's only fifteen but already knows everything about anything, "it's extremely rude for Sophia to count how many helpings of chicken pot pie Hannah had for dinner."

"Girls?"

That's all Mom has to say. Especially when she cocks her left eyebrow up half an inch and gives us . . .

"Your father already had dinner with some colleagues at the diner," says Mom.

"Good," says Hannah. "But if he's still hungry, he can have some of my fudge. I hid some under my pillow. . . ."

Yes, Hannah does that. A lot. Which is why, sometimes, she wakes up with melted chocolate in her ear.

"He's fine, honey," says Mom. "Your father and I need to see you all in the living room at nineteen hundred hours. Family meeting."

"Nineteen hundred hours" is military speak for 7:00 p.m. I glance at the kitchen clock. It's 6:46.

"Between now and then," says Mom, "finish your homework. Dis-*missed!*"

Everybody bustles out of the kitchen except Riley and me. Riley's eleven and is in the unfortunate position of being my next-younger sister. That means she looks up to me, which is not always the best or wisest move. (I wasn't exactly a super-duper role model when I was twelve. Okay, I was probably the worst role model ever. A dinner roll would've been a better role model.)

"What do you think's going on?" Riley asks.

"I don't know!" I pretend to panic. "The suspense is killing me. Literally!" I bring my hands up to my throat, bug out my eyes, and act like I've just swallowed poison, then collapse to the ground. "Gak! I'm dead! Killed by suspense."

Riley laughs.

I take a little bow.

"Don't worry," I say. "It's probably something good. Hey, maybe now that Mom is home, we're all going somewhere cool for a family vacation."

"Do you think it's Disney World?" gasps Riley, her eyes going wide.

She's been wanting to go to Disney World ever since she saw the New Kids on the Block *Wildest Dreams* special on TV. (FYI—New Kids on the Block were the big boy band back in the 1990s. They were sort of like whoever's replaced Justin Bieber and One Direction on your lunch boxes.)

"I hope so," I tell Riley.

Dad arrives home at 6:59, on the dot. We all assemble in the living room.

"Girls?" he says. "I have some terrific news."

"We're going to Disney World?" Riley blurts out,

sounding like a Super Bowl commercial.

"Not this summer, dear," says Mom. "Your father has a new job!"

"You're not going to head up the lifeguards?" I say.

"No, ma'am," says Dad, taking Mom's hand. "In fact, I am taking the first steps on the road to my dream job."

"You're going to be a cop?" gushes sweet Hannah. "Oh, Dad, that is so wonderful! All your hard work, all your studying, all your nights away from home . . ."

It's true. Dad worked really hard studying to take his police officer exam. So hard, we hardly ever saw him last fall. Some of us even got a little suspicious about where he was going all the time. (That would've been me.)

"Congratulations, Father," says Victoria.

"Woo-hoo!" I say, giving Dad a hearty arm pump.

Emma just races across the room and hugs his leg.

Dad laughs. "Thank you, ladies. I couldn't have done it without your support."

"And," says Mom, "he won't be able to continue

doing it without your continued support."

"That's right, girls," says Dad. "I know school's nearly over. That you all had big plans for the summer."

Uh-oh.

Dad just said "had." *As in, past tense.*

That means we probably shouldn't have them anymore.

CHAPTER 3

Seaside Heights, New Jersey, is a shore town.

That means, starting in June, when the tourists and day-trippers descend on our sandy beaches, the population will swell from the twenty-four hundred people who actually live here to the twenty or thirty thousand who come here to play, eat junk food, show off their tans, and cool off in the surf. That also means the police department needs some extra, summer-only help.

"I am now a Seasonal Class One officer with the Seaside Heights Police Department," Dad proudly announces.

"And," adds Mom, "if things go well this summer, we're pretty sure your father will be offered a full-time job on the force right after Labor Day."

"One seasonal officer typically is," says Dad, bouncing up on the balls of his feet like he's so happy he could burst. "My days of heading up the lifeguarding crew are over, ladies."

"Hoo-ah!" says Mom. Then they hug.

This was great news for Dad, also known as the best-looking boy on the beach. Mac Hart was inching closer to living his dream, doing the thing he wanted to do more than anything in the world—especially since his professional baseball career was cut short after he met Mom, hung up his cleats, and had seven kids, all girls. If Mom and Dad had played with us, we could have been our own softball team.

"Eventually," says Mom, "the police department job will give your father a nice salary."

"And benefits!" says Dad.

"But . . ."

Yep. There's always a *but.* And this *but* sounds like a big one.

" . . . this seasonal position will not pay well at all."

Dad nods. "The pay stinks."

"And there are no benefits," says Mom.

"Plus, I have to buy my own uniforms."

"What about your pistol?" asks Sophia. "Do you have to buy that, too?"

"Seasonal officers don't carry sidearms," says Dad. "Mostly, we write parking tickets. Help out with traffic congestion. Check beach badges. That sort of thing."

"And," says Mom, "because my dream is also to, one day, become a police officer, I have enrolled in an eight-week, intensive summer training program at the community college. Just like the one your father took last fall."

"So," says Dad, "your mother will not be pulling down a salary at all for two months."

"I won't be able to do as much cooking, cleaning, and childcare, either," she adds.

Now they both look at us.

"We need your help, kids," says Mom.

"We need you girls to find jobs this summer," says Dad. "All of you who are old enough to work need to bring home a steady paycheck."

"Otherwise," says Mom, "we may not be able to afford groceries."

Hannah gasps when she hears that. She likes to eat. Then again, so do I.

"We're also going to need some help in the babysitting department," says Dad, looking to Emma. She's six. No way is anybody hiring her this summer. At least, not legally. New Jersey has child labor laws. You have to be twelve to get your working papers.

"You girls will need to take turns looking after

your youngest sister," says Mom. "And walking Sandfleas."

Sandfleas is our dog. She's a girl, too.

"What about me?" asks Riley.

"You're eleven," says Dad. "You'll have to look after yourself and help around the house."

"And," says Mom, "if Jacky can't find a job, she can help you."

Great.

My lazy, hazy, crazy plans for the summer have just been put on hold. I'll either be working or I'll be the chief cook, floor scrubber, toilet swisher, and babysitter at home.

So much for fun in the sun.

CHAPTER 4

Mom and Dad were the first ones to tell me that "if you do what you love, you'll never work a day in your life."

Maybe not, but it sure sounded like us kids would have to work—every day during our so-called summer vacation.

"The shops and booths along the boardwalk are always hiring summer help," says Mom. "Plus, you can learn a lot holding down a job. It'll be a good experience for all of you."

"And," says Dad, "you can keep half of your take-home pay."

That sounds better.

"But," says Mom, "all allowances will forthwith be suspended until after Labor Day."

Okay. Maybe not so much.

Because if we want pocket change for ice cream, video games, CDs, movie tickets, popcorn, Slurpees, bubble gum, new swimsuits—all the essentials of summer life—we have to go out and earn it. Our ride on the Mom and Dad gravy train is over.

By the way, why would anybody want to haul gravy around on a train? What's up with that? Wouldn't the gravy slosh up and over the sides of the cargo cars?

Anyhow, the next day, it's back to school

The second I step through the front door, Ms. Katherine O'Mara, my favorite teacher, grabs me by the elbow.

"They need you in the office. Now!"

"Am I in trouble already?" I say. "How is that possible? It's not even eight thirty. . . ."

"Lauren Furtado is out sick," says Ms. O'Mara. "Mrs. Turner needs you to do the morning announcements."

Lauren Furtado is this girl from the debate squad who has super-duper diction and an incredible speaking voice. My guess? Lauren Furtado will be enunciating stuff on talk radio the second she graduates from college with a degree in Very Proper Public Speaking.

No way do I want to take her place.

"B-b-but . . ."

"No buts, Jacky," says Ms. O'Mara. "It's time for the understudy to go on."

"B-b-but c-c-couldn't y-y-you f-f-find s-s-someone else?"

That's right. When the pressure's on, I stutter.

Stuttering, of course, is how I got my nickname,

Jacky Ha-Ha. When I was in pre-K, my tongue would trip all over itself and mangle my own last name. My old enemy Bubblebutt, a beefy kid who's been a bully since he punched a Cabbage Patch Kid smack in the face in his baby days, heard me sputtering "Jacky Ha-Ha-Hart" during story time one afternoon and slapped the Jacky Ha-Ha label on me. It's been stuck there like a KICK ME sign ever since.

"You'll do fine, Jacky," says Ms. O'Mara. "You're every bit as talented as Lauren Furtado."

Ms. O'Mara was a speech and theater major in college. She also appeared in the Broadway production of *Annie* when she was a kid. She's helped me a lot, but the truth is whenever I have to do a cold reading (that's whenever I have to read aloud a bunch of words I haven't seen before or words I don't understand), I forget everything I know about controlling my speech impediment and I skitter off the rails into Stutterville again!

CHAPTER 5

Ms. O'Mara hurries me into the office.

Mrs. Turner, the assistant principal, who's also been very good to me, is standing there smiling. Holding a microphone. She gestures to me.

I shake my head. "I'm n-n-no L-L-Lauren F-F-Furtado."

"Oh, don't underestimate yourself, Jacqueline!" says Mrs. Turner. She forces the microphone into my hand.

"Good luck!" whispers Ms. O'Mara. "Just take your time and be you."

"Or Lauren Furtado," says Mrs. Turner, handing me the script. "Lauren's an excellent announcement reader. Just pretend you're her or she's you. . . ."

I look at the sheet of paper. It's filled with words, words, words. Words I have never seen before. Words I don't know how to pronounce.

One jumps out at me. On the birthday list I see an eighth grader named Debbie Swierczynski!

SWIERCZYNSKI!

What do all those consonants even sound like all smooshed together like that?

"You're on!" says Mrs. Turner.

My mouth is drier than it is after I eat a whole sleeve of saltines.

"Um, 'Good morning, starshine,'" I tell the microphone. "'The earth says hello....'"

Okay. I've been listening to a ton of Broadway musical albums in my room lately. That line is from a song in *Hair*. Yes, once upon a time, there was a whole Broadway show about hair. I'm still waiting for one about toenail clippings.

Reciting lines I've memorized is an easy way to avoid my stutter.

"Stick to the script, Jacqueline," whispers Mrs. Turner. "Lauren would."

I take a deep breath and try to remember all the stuff Ms. O'Mara taught me to tame my stutter. Her most important advice? Take your time.

"Good . . . mor . . . ning . . . Sea . . . side . . . Heights . . . Mid . . . dle . . . School."

I'm speaking slower than a turtle stuck in quicksand. I'm even taking pauses between syllables.

Mrs. Turner gives me the ol' spinning finger. The universal signal for *Let's speed things up, shall we?*

"H-h-happy b-b-birthday to . . ."

(That's what I call my anticipatory stutter. My mouth knows what's coming next and it isn't happy about it.)

". . . to . . . Deb-bie . . . S-S-Sewer . . . uh . . . Deb-bie Sw-sw-swerve . . . Sw-sw-sweerz . . . cuz-zzzzee . . . zzzin . . . zzzine . . . ska-nin-ski-zebra-ski-slope!"

My stutter makes me sputter as much spittle as a sprinkler!

Ms. O'Mara and Mrs. Turner are staring at me as if I'm a horror movie at the drive-in.

Or a car wreck.

Maybe both.

Fortunately, Ms. O'Mara isn't just my English teacher and mentor.

She's also my friend.

She sees the panic swirling in my eyes. She can probably also see the flop-sweat stains spiraling around the armpits of my blouse. Heck, everybody can see those. They're the size of Lake Erie.

She grabs the microphone.

"Jacky Hart?" she says. "You crack me up! You know how to pronounce Debbie's last name. . . ."

"I do? I mean, yes. I do."

"It's Swierczynski," says Ms. O'Mara perfectly.

"Exactly."

"But you couldn't resist doing a comic bit on it, could you?"

Ms. O'Mara nods at me. Okay. Now we're improvising a scene. I don't stutter when I'm playing a part in a scene. And the number one rule of improv is always to say yes and build on whatever your scene partner throws your way.

"Yeah. Sorry, Debbie. I wasn't making fun of your name. I was just kicking off our school-wide celebration of National Consonants Week."

"Yes, indeed," says Ms. O'Mara.

Now that I'm doing something I'm comfortable with, I'm on a roll and keep going. "We just wanted to alert everyone to the danger of bumping too many consonants up against each other. This week, lend them a vowel, if you have one to spare."

"Why, thank you, Jacky, for that very informative public service announcement."

"Brought to you by me and the Ad Council," I say, because I've heard announcers say that on TV.

Ms. O'Mara winks at me and takes over the real announcements.

Which is a good thing.

Because the next part is about the lunch menu. Creamy chipped beef on toast, corn, string beans, and a fruit cup.

Just reading that out loud might make me want to hurl.

CHAPTER 6

Ms. O'Mara finishes reading the morning's announcements.

"Now please rise and face the flag for the Pledge of Allegiance," she says.

I put my hand over my heart (which is racing faster than a rabbit being chased by a pack of dogs being chased by a dinosaur) and recite the pledge flawlessly.

Because I've memorized the words.

That's how I was able to play Snoopy in the fall musical and Essie in the spring comedy. I knew my lines. I had a character to hide behind. If I know what I'm doing, if I've rehearsed and prepared, if I'm improvising a comic bit with another actor, then I don't freak out. I don't stutter.

When the announcements are finished, Ms. O'Mara and I stroll up the hall together.

"Cold readings are always my least favorite, too," she says.

"I'm sorry. . . ."

"No, Jacky. *I'm* sorry. We shouldn't've asked you to jump in like that. I just thought it might be fun for you. Like being a disc jockey or doing a radio drama . . ."

"I didn't want to goof up and make a m-m-major m-m-mistake."

"Jacky, remember what we said about mistakes when you're onstage doing a show?"

"Unless you act like you goofed up, people in the audience, who haven't been to any rehearsals or read the script, will never even know that you made a mistake."

"Exactly. The same thing is true when you're doing a cold reading. If you act like you know what you're doing, no one will ever know if you don't. You have to fake it until you make it. For instance, everybody at this school thinks I'm actually a teacher because I *act* like a teacher. Truth be told, I never studied teaching in college. I was a high school drop-out. The only college I've ever attended is that one you see on TV where they teach you how to drive big-rig trucks."

"What?"

"Kidding. But I had you believing it because I acted like I believed it, too."

That makes me laugh.

"See you in class," says Ms. O'Mara as I stop at my locker.

"Okay. And I won't tell anybody you're a trucker, not a teacher."

"Good. It'll be our secret."

She takes off. I work my combination.

All of a sudden, out of the corner of my eye, I see Bubblebutt and his sidekick, Ringworm, sidling up the hall. They're both wearing black T-shirts with NIИ plastered across the front, for a heavy metal band named Nine Inch Nails.

Seriously. In 1991, that was a band, not something you bought at Home Depot if you were building a railroad.

Anyway, Bubblebutt is smiling.

Seeing Bubblebutt sauntering up the hall makes me nervous.

Like I said, he and Ringworm have been tormenting me since my *Sesame Street* and *Muppet Babies* days.

My guess?

He's here to make fun of me for stuttering through that birthday announcement!

CHAPTER 7

Bubblebutt gives Ringworm an elbow to the ribs, telling him to beat it.

As always, Ringworm does what Bubblebutt's elbow tells him to.

It's just me and Bubblebutt. Alone. I snuffle the air. Bubblebutt smells like a magazine with a scratch-and-sniff Obsession by Calvin Klein cologne ad tucked inside it. I think he rubbed his face in it.

He's smiling at me. Nicely.

What's he up to?

"Uh, hello, Bob," I say, because that's Bubblebutt's real name.

"Hey, Jacky."

I'm so used to him making fun of me that my

name sounds a little weird coming out of his mouth. I notice that he won't look right at me, either.

Strange. All of a sudden, he seems shy. Almost semihuman.

Weirder still, in that moment I don't absolutely despise him. Maybe all that Calvin Klein cologne wafting through the air is making me dizzy. Maybe I'm twelve and things about boys have started becoming a little more, what's the word I'm looking for?

Confusing? Complicated?

Yes. I am complicatedly confused. And Bob? All of a sudden, his perma-sneer seems sort of sweet, in that bad-boy, early-Elvis sort of way.

"Um, do you need something?" I ask.

"Yeah. Uh, first of all, hysterical birthday announcement this morning."

"Thanks."

"Is it really National Consonants Week?"

"Yes," I say. "Brought to you by all the letters except *A, E, I, O, U.*"

"Huh?"

"Sorry. That was a *Sesame Street* joke."

"Oh. Cool. You're funny, Jacky. I can't believe that, back in the day, I used to make fun of you."

"You mean last week?"

"Yeah. I was so stupid last week."

I don't disagree.

"Anyway," says Bob as he tries to dig a hole in the linoleum floor with the toe of his tennis shoe. "School's almost out. . . ."

"No it's not. It's not even first period. . . ."

"Ha! See? That was another funny joke. Seriously. You crack me up, Jacky. What I meant is that school's almost out for the summer."

"Yeah. . . ."

Where is this going? I'm wondering. Bob's train of thought is like a tin windup toy. You don't know where it'll go next, until it bumps into a wall.

"So," he says, "anyway . . ."

The boy can definitely hem and haw.

". . . I was sort of hoping that, this summer, that maybe you and me—maybe we could get into some trouble. We could, you know, go climb a Ferris wheel together or something. Pull some pranks. Punk some people. Or maybe we could just go see a movie."

I gulp.

Is Bubblebutt asking me out on a date? Does he suddenly have some kind of weird crush on me?

If he does, I have only two words for it:

Ewwww. And *gross!*

Then again . . .

He is kind of cute when he's being sweet.

And that Calvin Klein cologne he dunked his head into doesn't smell so bad.

Not bad at all.

So I tell Bob that I'm going to be kind of busy this summer.

"I need to find a summer job," I say with a sad shrug.

He nods grimly. "That's cool. I guess I'd do that, too, but nobody will hire me. Or if they did, they'd probably fire me, like, an hour later. I'm not what many consider prime employee material. . . ."

"Y-y-yeah," I say, slipping into a stutter because something about being alone with Bob makes me nervous.

"Nice chatting with you, Jacky. See you around. Good luck finding that job."

Wow. He didn't make fun of my stuttering or even call me Jacky Ha-Ha. Something weird is definitely going on inside that very large head of his.

And inside mine, too!

CHAPTER 8

I spend most of the day puzzling over this strange new Bob. Not that I talk to anybody about it. That would be even weirder.

I do think about discussing it with my mom. She might remember what it was like when she was my age. But these days she's so busy with cop school and being a mom to seven kids that it's hard to find alone time with her.

After school, I find Riley so we can ride our bikes home together. Bike rides are always good for clearing your head.

Actually, Riley rides a bike, I ride La Bicicletta.

I used to call my bike Le Bike, because it made

me feel, how you say, French. But, as zee summer approaches, I am feeling more Italian. You know—sunny and Mediterranean with a killer tan. I picture myself wearing big bug-eye sunglasses with white frames, my hair tucked under a scarf, my skirt billowing in the breeze, designer shopping bags draped over my handlebars, as I guzzle olive oil from a jug with a wicker basket bottom. And I do not need to pedal La Bicicletta because, in my mind, it is actually Il Vespa, a motor scooter.

Ciao, bella!
That means "Hello, beautiful," not "It's time for dinner, Bella."

Riding La Bicicletta (even an imaginary one) is way more fun than riding a boring old bike, which is what Riley and I are doing. It's one of the many advantages of a vivid imagination. Use your imagination, and anything can become interesting. Like doing dishes . . . just pretend your hands are scuba diving in the sudsy ocean and bringing up buried treasure instead of scraping fish bones off a plate.

We take a shortcut along the Seaside Heights boardwalk, which is starting to show signs of life as it gears up for the summer season. There are all sorts of food stands, serving everything from pizza to swirl cones to Italian sausage sandwiches smothered in peppers and onions. If you love having heartburn or acid indigestion, this is the place to eat.

There are also thrill rides and games of chance where you can waste a ton of money trying to win a stuffed pink gorilla for your girlfriend (but then you have to lug the gigantic toy around the boardwalk with you for the rest of the day and into the night).

And don't forget the video arcades and fortune-tellers and clubs where loud music spills out the doors all night long.

It's a teen paradise.

Too bad I'm not a teen.

I'm just twelve and I need to find a summer job.

So much fun in one location! Too bad fun is officially canceled for the Hart family this summer.

Actually, as Riley and I pedal along, past the blinking lights, the sizzling cheesesteaks, and the signs that say NO BICYCLES ALLOWED, I realize that a summer job on the boardwalk may not be horrible.

Sure, I'll come home smelling like I've been

dipped in batter and deep-fried with the Mars bars, but working in a food stall isn't as hard as, I don't know, coal mining or something. And if I can land a job at the Ringtoss, Frog Bog, or Pop-a-Balloon booth, I might earn a few laughs along with my paycheck.

This is what I'm thinking when, all of a sudden, a pair of police officers step out of the shadows to raise their hands, signaling for Riley and me to freeze right where we are.

Uh-oh.

CHAPTER 9

"Can't you girls read?" asks a gruff police officer.

He has gray hair that's been buzz-cut into a bristle-brush flattop. He also wears mirrored sunglasses.

"Didn't you see that 'No Bicycles Allowed' sign back there?"

"Yes, sir," I say, resisting the urge to add something a little more smart-alecky, like *And didn't you see what your hair looked like before you paid your barber?*

Because the other cop isn't just any old Seasonal Class One officer working the boardwalk beat with Officer Flattop.

The other cop is *Dad.*

Officer Flattop gives us a lecture and lets us off with a warning. Dad pretends he doesn't know Riley or me.

I can't blame him.

His chances of being offered a full-time job will probably go down the toilet with a very loud *WHOOSH!* if his superior officers ever find out that his two daughters are complete juvenile delinquents who regularly break the Seaside Heights no-bicycles-on-the-boardwalk law.

And no, that's not the big mistake I made that summer, because, officially, summer hadn't even started yet. My whopper was yet to come. Patience, girls, patience.

Anyway, Dad and his partner stroll up the boardwalk. Riley and I push our bikes in the opposite direction.

"Do you think Dad is going to start giving us tickets when we do something wrong at home?" asks Riley.

"No," I say. "That's Mom's job."

"She doesn't give us tickets."

"She doesn't have to. She just has to give us the Look."

I cock my left eyebrow halfway up my forehead and scowl at Riley, doing a pretty decent Mom impression.

"Hoo-ah!" I bellow, the way a marine would if there were a monster under somebody's bed.

Riley laughs, which makes me smile. I think our recent run-in with the law upset her more than it did me.

"I'm so glad Mom is home safe," says Riley. "Even if she does give us the Look."

“Me too,” I say, because I am.

We were all worried sick when Mom was over in the Middle East. When your mother is a soldier and goes off to do her job and actually fight in a real war, there’s always a chance that she won’t come home when that job is done. We did a lot of praying when Big Sydney Hart was stationed in Saudi Arabia. We do a lot of praying now that she’s home, too. But these are the happy prayers. The ones where you say, “Thank you, thank you, thank you, thank you, thank you!”

We pass a giant fiberglass ice cream cone and a souvenir shop (with stuff like FBI: FULL-BLOODED ITALIAN printed on the T-shirts), then come to a whole cluster of game booths. There’s a Wheel of Fortune, a Baseball Toss, a Whack-a-Mole, and a Balloon Race. The Balloon Race is the goofiest because you aim your squirt gun at a clown’s tiny mouth. When you nail the target with your water jet, a balloon over the clown’s head inflates. First balloon to pop wins.

As fun as that sounds, the guy running the balloon race sounds totally bored.

“Win a Tweety for your sweetie,” he drones into his microphone. “Take home a Bart to your sweetheart. Nothing says ‘I love you’ like Winnie the Pooh.”

He limply gestures toward the stuffed Tweety Bird, Bart Simpson, and Winnie the Pooh prizes dangling off a pegboard behind him.

I hate to say it, but the guy in the booth is terrible at his job. He's driving customers away in hordes.

"I'm going home," says Riley. "It's my turn to babysit Emma."

"I'll be right behind you," I tell her.

Because I can't resist.

The busker in me (*busker* is a fancy word for "street performer") wants to pop behind the counter and show the Balloon Race guy how you drum up a crowd!

CHAPTER 10

In case you haven't heard (or forgot), I can pull some pretty crazy stunts and practical jokes.

For instance, I climbed the Seaside Heights Ferris wheel. Twice.

I got Bill Phillips to eat chewing gum soaked in hot sauce. The four-fireball variety.

And then there's this other thing I did once with shaving cream that I'm definitely not even going to mention because you'd probably do it to everyone if I did!

It's like I have this devil on my shoulder, poking and prodding me to do wild and crazy stuff while the angel on my other shoulder is taking a nap or watching music videos on MTV.

"Excuse me," I say to the sleepy-eyed, Italian-looking guy who is, once again, reciting the first stanza of his lame rhymes.

"Yeah? You want to play?"

"Yes."

"You want to win a Tweety for your sweetie?"

"Not exactly. I want to play with your microphone."

"Huh?"

"Look, Vinnie," I say, reading his name tag, "you

don't have any customers. And you know why?"

"Because you kids are scared of clowns on account of that Stephen King book, am I right?"

"No. It's because your pitch isn't exactly pitch perfect. You've got the steak, but you forgot to add any sizzle."

"What? You think you could do better, kid?"

I show Vinnie my thumb and index finger with just a sliver of space between them. "Little bit."

"Fine. Knock yourself out, kid. En-*joy*." He hands me the microphone. "I wanted to go grab a slice of pizza anyways. Haven't eaten for two hours. I'm starving here. . . ."

Yes, he actually hands me the microphone and deserts his booth.

I feel the same rush of adrenaline I always feel right before I go on. It shoots up into my head, tickles my nose, and tingles my toes. It's the best feeling in the world, I kid you not.

It's *showtime.*

First I have to get into character, because if I don't, we're in for a repeat of the school announcements and Debbie Swierczynski! My character of choice? The classic carnival barker! Or circus ringmaster. Maybe a combination platter.

"Ladies and gentlemen, boys and girls, step right up!" I say to the crowd walking by the Balloon Race booth. "One of these clowns is about to go down. We're going to burst his bubble! Say, do you know what happened to the circus lion after he ate a clown? He felt funny! Do you know what they call that gooey red stuff between a circus elephant's toes? Slow clowns!"

I riff on every corny clown joke I've ever heard, then I move on to balloon bashing.

"Don't you think balloons are weird? It's like, 'Happy birthday. Here's a plastic bag full of my breath.' What a great gift! They're like a whoopee cushion on a string. *Pbbbbt!*"

Before long, I have a huge crowd. Every water pistol on the firing line is manned.

People are handing me fistfuls of money.

Vinnie strolls back, wrestling with his slimy slice of grease-dribbling pizza.

"I'll take that," he says when he sees the wad of cash I just raked in. I fork it over, of course. (Come on, that devil on my shoulder isn't *that* devilish!)

Vinnie flicks the switch that rings the bells and pumps water through the squirt guns.

While the shooters laugh and have a blast spraying their clown targets, Vinnie turns to me.

"You got talent, kid. Real talent. You were born to be a carnie. How'd you like a job this summer?"

Now, all of a sudden, the angel on my shoulder is wide awake, telling me to say yes immediately and take the job because that's exactly what Mom and Dad need me to do.

"Sure," I say. "Once school's out."

Vinnie and I shake on it.

And that's how yours truly, Jacky Hart, landed her first full-time, professional, moneymaking job in show business, at a balloon-popping booth on the boardwalk in Seaside Heights.

Making $3.80 an hour.

I was going to be a millionaire!

Right after I worked 263,158 hours.

CHAPTER 11

It's the last period on the last day of school.

The unofficial start of summer is just one jangling bell away.

In my head, I'm already singing that Alice Cooper song "School's Out," but I'm not wearing half as much makeup as Mr. Cooper.

In reality, a place I unfortunately have to visit from time to time, I'm hanging out in Ms. O'Mara's Honors English class with my buds from the drama club: Dan Napolitano (actor), Jeff Cohen (funny guy), Meredith Crawford (my BFF and an excellent singer), and Bill Phillips (he of the gorgeous hazel eyes).

Bob/Bubblebutt isn't in this class. That's probably

a good thing. I'm not sure what kind of belly flops my stomach might start doing if Bill and Bob were in the same room. It'd be a battle of hazel eyes against bad-boy smirk.

Since it's the last day of school, we're supposed to be killing time watching a VHS tape on the VCR.

(It was 1991, girls. Streaming hadn't been invented yet. We didn't even have DVDs! If you wanted to watch a movie, you had to slide a clunky videocassette the size of a math book into the mouth of a machine that sometimes chewed the tape like it was magnetic spaghetti.)

But nobody is interested in movie watching. We've all already seen *Honey, I Shrunk the Kids* and *Look Who's Talking*, the only two tapes Ms. O'Mara has in her classroom collection, besides, of course, her mountain of BBC Shakespeare tapes.

And NOBODY wants to watch those.

"I'm going to be working in the Balloon Race booth," I announce.

"Where you shoot the clown with the water pistol?" says Jeff.

"Yeah."

"Clowns are so creepy," says Dan.

“I know,” I tell him. “That’s why people like to shoot them in the mouth.”

“I got a job in the T-shirt shop,” says Bill with a grin.

Did I mention he has two extremely cute dimples? If only he smelled like Bob and Calvin Klein. The cologne, not the guy.

Meredith, who moved to Seaside Heights from Newark last year, found a job making meatball subs and cheese fries.

“Mmm,” I say. “I know where I’m having lunch every day. . . .”

“Well,” says Jeff, “I’m still waiting to hear, but, fingers crossed, I think I might’ve landed my dream job.”

“What is it?” asks Dan.

“Don’t want to jinx it by talking about it. Let’s just say it’s dairy related.”

“But you’re lactose intolerant,” says Bill.

“Doesn’t matter. This is the sweetest summer job on the boardwalk.”

Ms. O’Mara drifts through the door, a big smile on her face.

“Sorry I’m late, you guys,” she says. “I thought you’d be watching a movie. . . .”

“We’ve seen them all,” says Dan.

“Even my vast collection of Shakespeare videos?”

“Ewwww,” we all say. Together. Then we make assorted *Gag me with a spoon* gestures.

“You guys?” says Ms. O’Mara with a laugh. “Shakespeare is the best.”

“Definitely,” says Jeff. “Especially when you need to take a nap. Best sleeping pill ever invented . . .”

“‘Lord, what fools these mortals be!’” says Ms. O’Mara with a head shake and a sigh.

To sleep
or not to sleep.
There is no question.
But if thou
snoozeth,
thou
loseth.

“Huh?” says Dan.

“That’s Shakespeare,

Dan. In fact, it's from a play I thought some of you might want to be in this summer. With a cast of professional actors from New York City, including several Broadway stars. You'd be performing in front of a *huge* audience—bigger than anything we had for all our school shows combined."

Okay.

Broadway stars? Huge audience?

She definitely has our attention!

CHAPTER 12

Some friends of mine from New York—old Broadway buddies—are starting the first-ever Shakespeare Down the Shore festival right here in Seaside Heights. They're putting together a cast right now," Ms. O'Mara tells us.

"Why do they need kid actors?" I ask.

"Because their inaugural show is *A Midsummer Night's Dream*. Some of the cast needs to be youthful, unlike old dinosaurs like me."

"Are you going to be in it?"

"Hello? It's Shakespeare! They've asked me to play Titania, the queen of the fairies. So I suggested we audition you guys to be my supporting cast."

"Huh?" says Dan.

"Puck, Peaseblossom, Cobweb, Moth, and Mustardseed."

"Huh?" This time Bill says it.

"They're the fairy queen's fairies."

Jeff blushes. Clears his throat. "You want me to play a *fairy?*"

Okay, where's Pinocchio? Did a woodpecker get him?

"If it helps," says Ms. O'Mara, "don't call them fairies, Jeff. Call them shrewd and knavish sprites or merry wanderers of the night."

"Oh. Okay. Cool. That's better."

"That's what Shakespeare calls them," Ms. O'Mara explains.

"I know," I say. "That's why we couldn't understand what you were saying about Sprite. I like 7UP better."

Everybody laughs.

"Auditions aren't until the weekend," says Ms. O'Mara. "So you have some time to think about it. But it would be such a blast to do a show with you guys. You're all so good onstage."

"True," says Jeff. "We're all that and a bag of chips."

"Where are they doing the play?" asks Dan.

Ms. O'Mara smiles. "On the beach, on the same stage as the music fest."

"No way," says Jeff. "That thing is huge."

"I know. And there's nothing better than doing Shakespeare outdoors under the stars. We're scheduled between the Battle of the Bands and the

Southside Johnny concert. My friends have already sold, like, a thousand tickets!"

I raise my hand.

"Yes, Jacky?"

"Are the fairies funny?"

"Definitely. Especially Puck. He's very . . . puck-ish! You know, playful in a mischievous way."

Hmmm, I think. *Sounds like me. Especially when that little devil is whispering in my ear.*

"Is that where the word *puckish* comes from?" asks Bill. "From Puck?"

"Yes," says Ms. O'Mara. "We get a lot of modern sayings from Shakespeare. 'Forever and a day.' 'Heart of gold.' 'In a pickle.'"

"Oooh," says Jeff. "All of a sudden, I'm hungry."

The bell rings. It's the last bell for the last period on the last day of school!

Ms. O'Mara looks a little sad.

"'Parting is such sweet sorrow,'" she says.

"More Shakespeare?" I ask.

She nods.

It's weird. None of us want to dash out the door, even though the last day of school rivals Christmas morning on the I-can't-wait-for-it scale.

But not this year.

“Wh-wh-when are those auditions a-g-g-gain?” I ask.

“Saturday. They’re posting notices at the high school, too.”

“W-w-we’ll think about it,” I say.

“Yeah,” says Bill, looking at me with a worried look.

In fact, everybody is looking at me worriedly because, all of a sudden, I’m stuttering again.

Yep. Just thinking about Shakespeare, with all his strange and mysterious words, will do that to you.

Well, to me, anyway.

CHAPTER 13

The very next morning, on the first day of what was supposed to be my summer vacation, I report for duty at the Balloon Race booth.

I was also in charge of making sure Emma had breakfast. She wanted pizza. Cheese pizza. Good thing we had some in the fridge.

Since school's out, mobs of middle school, high school, and college kids are already cruising up and down the boardwalk.

"Okay, Funny Girl," says Vinnie, rubbing his tiny hands together like a greedy raccoon. "Here come the suckers. Start reeling them in."

My new boss likes to wear a white tank top and a thick gold necklace with a medallion the size of a hood ornament dangling from its ropy chain. I think he also combs his back hair.

Anyway, he leans back against a wall, wrapping his arms around a tin money box like he's hugging it.

I start my spiel with a little riff on an old Motown hit. "Ladies and gentlemen, there's nothing worse than the tears of a clown when people shoot him in the face with squirt guns. Bozo goes bananas. It's pop-goes-the-weasel time. Step right up. Pretend it's Ronald McDonald and he won't tell you what's in a Big Mac's secret sauce. . . ."

We do a very brisk morning business.

"Take a lunch break, kid," Vinnie tells me around one. "You earned it. I already doubled the take from yesterday when youse was at school."

I meet Meredith and Bill at the pizza place that's sort of in between all our jobs. We each grab a slice and a cup of soda on ice.

"How was your morning?" I ask.

"Slow," says Meredith. "Nobody really wants meatball subs and cheese fries for breakfast."

"I sold five T-shirts," says Bill. "Three that said 'Stupid.' Two with the finger pointing sideways that said 'I'm with Stupid.'"

"Guess one of the 'Stupids' really was," I quip.

"Definitely."

We're all stuffing pizza into our mouths when, surprise, Ms. O'Mara comes over to our picnic table balancing a red plastic tray. She's having a calzone, which is sort of like a slice of pizza folded over on top of itself.

"Hey, guys," she says.

"Um, what are you doing here?" I ask.

She shrugs. "School's out. I had the day off. I'm on vacation for two whole months. Thought I should eat some vacation food, which, by the way, is ten times better than cafeteria food. I also wanted to talk to you guys some more about the Shakespeare show."

I lean back and fake a huge, arm-stretching yawn. "Bo-rrring . . ."

Bill and Meredith giggle.

"Jacky," says Ms. O'Mara, pulling a funny frown face, "you're not giving poor Bill a chance. Don't say he's boring."

"Do you think I'm boring, Jacky?" says Bill.

"Of course not. You're, you know . . . practical."

"Isn't that another word for boring?"

"You guys?" says Ms. O'Mara. "I meant Bill as in William as in Shakespeare. For instance, did you know that in Shakespeare's day, he had to make everybody in his whole audience happy? From the rich nobles up in the galleries to the lowly groundlings down in the pit."

"What are groundlings?" asks Meredith. "Are they like Gremlins?"

"I love that movie," I say.

"Groundlings," says Ms. O'Mara, "were rowdy theatergoers who paid a penny to stand on the ground at the foot of the stage while the more, shall we say, sophisticated folks sat upstairs in cushioned seats. The richer you were, the higher your box seat. And if Shakespeare didn't make the groundlings laugh, guess what happened?"

"He felt terrible," I say, because that's how I feel when I tell a joke and nobody even chuckles.

"I'm sure he did. But his actors had it worse. They had to dodge a barrage of rotten fruit and vegetables."

"Seriously?" says Bill.

"Yep," says Ms. O'Mara. "If Shakespeare's audience didn't like his shows, they let him know it. They voted with their produce."

HUZZAH!
FREE CHOPPED SALAD
FOR ALL!
Before there was a movie website there were real ROTTEN TOMATOES

CHAPTER 14

Ms. O'Mara fills our lunch break with all sorts of interesting stuff about theater back in Shakespeare's day.

She tells us how all the girls' parts were played by boys with high-pitched voices, since girls weren't allowed to act back then. How the plays had to be performed during the day while the sun shone, since electricity and theatrical lighting hadn't been invented yet. How, since there was very little scenery, the audience had to fill in the blanks by using their imagination. How there was a trapdoor in the stage floor for quick exits and entrances.

Shakespeare is starting to sound pretty cool. An old-fashioned version of a savvy street performer who knows how to keep his audience hooked and stop them from growing restless.

But then I remembered my main stumbling block.

The w-w-words. Shakespeare's plays are filled with w-w-words I don't recognize or understand. Words that will definitely trip up my tongue and send me sputtering into a stupid stutter. If I do the show with Ms. O'Mara, I'll turn into Jacky Ha-Ha-Hart all over again.

"Fairy auditions are at two o'clock on Saturday," Ms. O'Mara tells us. "I really hope you guys will be there. I know Travis Wormowitz will."

"Um, who's this Travis Wormowitz?"

"Star of the high school drama club," says Ms. O'Mara. "He's super-psyched about playing Puck in a show with a professional cast. I don't know if he has the comedy chops for it, although I hear he was pretty funny in the high school musical, *Bye Bye Birdie*. Plus, if he's the only one auditioning for the part . . ."

O-kay.

Now my competitive juices are starting to flow.

"Jacky should be Puck!" says Bill.

"Definitely!" adds Meredith.

"Does Puck have to talk a lot?" I ask.

"Not a ton, but he has some great speeches," says Ms. O'Mara. "'Thou speakest aright: / I am that merry wanderer of the night. / I jest to Oberon, and make him smile / When I a fat and bean-fed horse beguile. . . .'"

From the lines Ms. O'Mara's reciting, it sounds like Shakespeare is making a fart joke. Why else would you feed beans to a horse?

But w-w-words like "m-m-merry w-w-wanderer"?

"I d-d-don't know."

That's when a cow comes wobbling over to our table.

"Ah'll eee ooo on aturay, mizz mamara!" says the guy in a cow costume. (And you thought they only said "moo.")

"Huh?" says Bill, because somebody had to.

"Ah'll eee ooo on aturay!"

"What?" says Ms. O'Mara.

Nobody can understand a word the cow is saying because the head is made out of thick papier-mâché.

"Ah'll eee aaht duh eye outs!" The way he's wiggling his belly, maybe he wants us to buy him a milk shake.

Quick, call Texas. We need someone who speaks Cow.

CHAPTER 15

The guy inside the cow costume stops talking and tries to heave off his head with his huge cow hooves because he's figured out that it's totally muffling his voice.

He wrestles with the cow head. He's twisting and turning so much, he looks like he's inventing a new dance—the funky cow. There's a lot of wiggling, but he can't get the costume piece to budge.

"Hang on," says Bill. "There's a hook around back. It's rusty."

I lend a hand. So does Meredith. We also lend our feet. It's hard to get a grip on a furry cow suit, especially with a wiggly person inside.

Finally, working together, the three of us are able to remove the cow head (without removing the head of the guy inside).

"Thanks!" says a very sweaty Jeff Cohen. His curly hair is soaked like a wet Brillo pad.

"Um, Jeff?" I say. "What's with the cow costume?"

"I got the job!"

"What job?"

"Ladies and gentlemen, you are looking at the new Bossy D. Cow for Swirl Tip Cones. *Moi!* Or, should I say, 'Moo!'"

"And *this* is your dream job?" I ask.

"Of course it is!" says Jeff. "It's showbiz, Jacky. I'm on all day. People love me. I'm a star. Kids want to shake my hoof wherever I roam. Plus, I get free ice cream on all my breaks."

"But you're lactose intolerant," I remind him. "Wouldn't that give you gas?"

"Yeah. It does get kind of stinky inside this suit from time to time."

"Yeah," says Bill, waving the air under his nose. "Maybe we should put that headpiece back on."

"No!" jokes Jeff. "I had a bean burrito for lunch! I'm dying in here." He waddles over to Ms. O'Mara. "Is Travis Wormowitz really going to be there? At the *Midsummer* auditions?"

"So I've heard," says Ms. O'Mara.

"Yeah. Me too. These high school girls were getting a free sample of Moose Tracks from me, and they were going gaga over this Travis guy. Guess he's been the star of every high school show since, like, forever."

"He's been going to high school since forever?" I say. "Do they keep holding him back? Maybe freshman algebra was a little too tough for Mr. Wormowitz.

And let's be honest, if the guy really wants to be an actor, he really needs to change his name. If he's a Wormowitz, all he can do is fish bait commercials on TV."

Jeff ignores me. "Count me in, Ms. O'Mara. If a high school superstar like Travis Wormowitz is going to be doing Shakespeare with you guys this summer, then that's what I want to be doing, too! I'll be there at the audition on Saturday."

"Is *that* what you were saying?" asks Ms. O'Mara.

"Yeah."

Aha! So *that's* what "Ah'll eee ooo on aturay, mizz mamara!" means in Cowese.

CHAPTER 16

I'm still torn first thing Saturday morning.

I'm at home, stirring my Froot Loops, watching the milk turn into a swirling paisley of colors, and trying to decide whether I want to go to the auditions for *A Midsummer Night's Dream*.

I'd love to be in the Shakespeare show with a bunch of professional Broadway actors and my middle school theater buds. Especially if it means I could play an awesome part like Puck.

I'd also love to beat out this high school hotshot Travis Wormowitz for the primo Puck role.

But I'm not even sure I could say W-W-Worm-o-w-w-witz at the audition if it's a cold reading (that means without practicing first) and my nerves kick in.

I guess I could've gone to the library one day after work and copied Puck's lines from the play to practice them. But I was having way too much fun hanging out with Meredith and Bill on the boardwalk. You'd be surprised how many times I went on the pirate ship ride without wanting to walk the plank.

At the time, I figured I could just wing it at the audition. *If* I decided to go.

Now I'm not so sure.

Plus, I'm supposed to babysit Emma this afternoon and work at the Balloon Race booth after that. I don't stutter when I'm on the job because I'm playing a role: the fast-talking boardwalk carnival barker.

Yes, Puck would be a role, too. But it would be a *SHAKESPEAREAN* role.

While I'm doing my own personal Hamlet bit—*To audition, or not to audition: that is the question*—the phone rings.

Victoria brings me the receiver, which is tethered to the kitchen wall by a long, sproingy cord. (In those days, our phones weren't smart. They were actually sort of dumb and anchored to the walls with cords.)

"It's for you, Jacqueline," reports Victoria, who, as you might recall, is fifteen going on fifty. "I believe it's your boyfriend. William Phillips!"

"Bill's not my boyfriend," I say, grabbing the phone and covering the mouthpiece so Bill can't hear me say it. "He's just a friend who happens to be a boy."

"Jacqueline," says Victoria with an exasperated huff, "I know a thing or two about L-O-V-E. I've read a ton of romance novels. Did you know that the average age for a first crush is—"

"Don't you have to go to work?" I say to Victoria.

"Yes. They have me running the taffy-pulling machine at the Taffy Shoppe. It's the most important job in the whole store, you know. I'm right there in the front window where all the tourists can watch me. As Mr. Willy Williams himself says, 'When you're in the window, you *are* Willy B. Williams's Taffy Shoppe.' And—"

"Hello?" I say to Bill, cutting her off.

"Hey. You ready to go to that audition?"

"I have to babysit Emma."

"Get Riley to take your slot."

"I dunno. . . ."

"Tell her you'll pull a double for her next weekend."

"But I have to go to work at the booth this afternoon. . . ."

"The auditions are in a church basement, like, a block away from the boardwalk."

"But—"

"That guy Wormowitz is going to be there. Are you gonna let him get the part without even trying? Besides, William Shakespeare just called. He wants *you* to play Puck, not some high school guy."

Yes, Bill Phillips was very persuasive, even back in 1991. It's why he's such a good lawyer today.

"Fine," I say. "I'll meet you there. And, Bill?"

"Yeah?"

"Pick up some rotten produce on the way. Maybe a stinky cabbage and a couple of wrinkled tomatoes."

"What for?"

"If we don't like this high school kid's performance, we can give him the old-fashioned groundling treatment!"

I seal the babysitting-swap deal with Riley. It's not a very good deal. I think I said yes to watching Emma when I'm also supposed to be at work. *Oh, well,* I decide, *I'll jump off that bridge when I come to it.* Who knows? Emma might have fun with the squirt guns and balloons.

Bill, Jeff, Dan, and Meredith meet me outside the church.

"Wormowitz is in there right now," reports Dan.

"He's reading for Puck," says Jeff.

"Puck's the best part for a kid," says Bill.

"And you're the best actress at Seaside Heights Middle School, Jacky," says Meredith.

"Actually, I'm more of a comedian. . . ."

"And Puck's supposed to be funny!"

"Not as funny as a cow," says Jeff. "Cows can do more slapstick shtick and moo puns. 'You look moovalous. Simply moovalous, darling . . .'"

"Shhh!" whispers Dan, gesturing toward an open window behind a dusty clump of dead weeds. It opens into the basement. "We can hear his audition!"

We huddle together and spy into the audition room below.

I can see Ms. O'Mara at a long table with three or four very theatrical-looking people. One of them has a goatee. Another one is in a black turtleneck sweater. In June.

The high school superstar is auditioning for the table, doing one of Puck's major speeches.

With any luck, I'll be your Puck and we can play goosey, goosey, duck, duck, duck.
Um. That's not Shakespeare, Mr. Wormowitz.
I know. It's pure me.

The guy finally gets around to doing the Puck speech the judges want to hear. "'Through bog, through bush, through brake, through briar. . .'"

Yes, it has a lot of *b-b-b*'s in it.

And Tr-Tr-Travis is good.

Really good.

But I don't care.

I'm going to go down there and be b-b-better!

CHAPTER 17

Let's go," I say.

"Home?" asks Bill.

"No. Downstairs. The auditions have already started!"

"Booyah!" says Jeff. "Or, you know, *moo*-yah!"

"Are you going to stay in cow character all summer long?" asks Dan with an eye roll.

"Probably. Do you have some kind of *beef* with that?"

We all groan.

"Okay, Jeff," I say. "We've *herd* enough puns. . . ."

"Yeah," says Bill. "Stop milking it, dude."

We all crack up. My friends are the best.

"Come on, you guys," says Meredith. "Unlike

Jeff's *cheesy* jokes, these auditions won't last all day."

She leads the way into the church and down the steps to the basement.

We all nearly have a heart attack.

Not from running down the steps too fast, but from who we see sitting behind a card table in front of the auditions door. It's Latoya Sherron.

The Latoya Sherron.

The beautiful actress who starred on Broadway in all sorts of shows, like *Dreamgirls* and *Ain't Misbehavin'*. She's also a huge pop star and has even danced in a couple of MC Hammer videos.

We all stand there with our mouths hanging open for probably five minutes.

Awkward.

"Um, hey," says Ms. Sherron. "Are you guys here for the auditions?"

"Yes, ma'am," says Bill.

"Are you in the show?" asks Meredith.

Ms. Sherron nods. "I'm playing Hippolyta, queen of the Amazons."

(No, girls. Hippolyta was not the queen of online shopping. The Internet wasn't really a thing in 1991. The Amazons were the original girl group, except they fought instead of singing.)

"Then sign us up!" I blurt out, because I'm super-excited even to have a shot at being in a show with a superstar like Latoya Sherron.

She holds a finger up to her lips. We *are* being kind of loud. And Travis Wormowitz is still on the other side of the door behind Ms. Sherron, auditioning for my part!

"Great," says Ms. Sherron, sliding a sign-up sheet across her card table toward us. "Are you Kathy's kids?"

"Who's Kathy?" asks Jeff.

"Ms. O'Mara," I say. "Her first name is Katherine."

"Really?" says Dan. "I thought it was, you know, Miz."

Ms. Sherron laughs a little. "Kathy and I were in *Annie* together, a long, long time ago. Just put your names on the sheet there and write down what role you're most interested in playing."

"Just a fairy," says Meredith, writing down her information.

"Can you sing?" asks Ms. Sherron.

"A little bit."

"She's being modest," I say. "Meredith is the best singer at Seaside Heights Middle School."

"Wonderful," says Ms. Sherron. "We might add some music and lyrics for the fairies. . . ."

Meredith slides the clipboard over to me.

I write down my name and the character I'm most interested in playing: Puck!

Ms. Sherron sees that.

"Would you be willing to play one of the smaller roles?" she asks.

"Well, Puck is my first choice. . . ."

"I understand. It's a great part." She nods her head toward the door. "But from what I've been hearing, we might already have our Puck."

"W-W-Worm-o-w-w-witz?" I sputter.

"Yeah. He's good. Memorized all the major monologues. Says he spent the whole week working on his audition."

I fake a queasy smile.

M-m-memorizing m-m-monologues?

Heck, I haven't even read *A Midsummer Night's Dream*! All I know about Puck is his name. For all I know, he's a guy who plays hockey.

Looks like I might have blown my audition before I even started.

CHAPTER 18

"Wait here," says Ms. Sherron, grabbing the sign-up sheet clipboard. "I'll let them know you guys are waiting."

She opens the door to the audition room. We can hear Travis Wormowitz winding up his audition.

"If we shadows have offended,
Think but this, and all is mended,
That you have but slumber'd here
While these visions did appear.
And this weak and idle theme,
No more yielding but a dream . . ."

The door closes, cutting off the rest of his speech.

"Wow," says Bill. "He's pretty good."

I shoot him a look.

"But, you know, not as good as you'll be, Jacky."

On the outside, I'm smiling. Inside, I'm wondering what Bob (aka Bubblebutt) might've said. Would he have been more supportive? More encouraging? He'd definitely smell better than Bill because Bob would've dunked his head in another bucket of that Calvin Klein cologne. Bill kind of smells like French fries. The T-shirt shop where he works is next door to a hot dog and crinkle cut stand.

Then I wonder why I'm even wondering about Bob when I should be thinking about Puck and the audition I am totally unprepared for.

The door swings open again.

"Thank you, kind sirs and madams!" Wormowitz says to the adults at the table as he, dramatically, backs out of the room. "It would be such an honor to work with each and every one of you! Parting is such sweet sorrow! Adieu! Adieu! I bid you adieu!"

The door closes in front of him.

"Why's he yammering about Mountain Dew?" asks Dan.

I shrug. I haven't a clue.

Mr. If I may quote Shakespeare: "Nothing can seem foul to those that win." And guess what: I just Won!
Must be why he seems so FOUL.

"Oh. Hello, kiddies," he says when he sees us. He's oozing an air of superiority that doesn't smell nearly as good as that Calvin Klein stuff. "Are you guys here to audition for some of the other fairies, the bit parts? Because I'm pretty sure the leading role of Puck is already taken. I nailed it!"

He raises a hand for a high five.

Nobody offers him a palm.

"Jacky's still got a shot," says Meredith, because she's my best friend.

"Who's Jacky?"

"M-m-me," I say.

"Oh, my," says Wormowitz. "What a w-w-way you have with w-w-words!"

"Knock it off, pal!" says Bill. "Don't make fun of Jacky!"

Wormowitz holds up both hands in surrender. "Well, *excuuuuse* me," he says. "I was just being puckish."

"Well," says Jeff. "Jacky can do that, too. She can be puckish. That's why they call these 'auditions.' They see additional people."

"Um, wouldn't those be called 'additions'?" says

Bill, because he's super-logical that way.

Wormowitz fixes his snooty gaze on Meredith. "Why, pray tell, are you even here, young lady? Black people weren't allowed onstage in Shakespeare's day."

YOUCH.

Did he just insult my best friend?

"Latoya Sherron is black," I snarl. My stutter doesn't dare show itself when I'm angry like this.

"No," sneers Wormowitz. "Ms. Sherron is a superstar. There's a difference. Good luck in there, little guys. Ciao for now."

He breezes up the steps.

"I just met him but I already hate him," says Dan.

"Ditto," says Jeff.

"Are you okay?" I ask Meredith.

"Seriously?" she says. "You think I'm gonna let some high school knuckle-dragging Neanderthal get under my skin? No way. And don't you let him get into your head, either, Jacky."

"I won't."

The five of us march into the audition room.

"Hi, guys!" says Ms. O'Mara from her seat behind

a long cafeteria-type table filled with paper, notepads, and pencils. There are four other grown-ups behind the table, including Latoya Sherron, who's talking to the guy with the goatee.

"Travis was good, huh?" I hear her say.

Mr. Goatee nods. "Fantastic. He'll be hard to beat."

I try to remember the speech Wormowitz recited. That bit about shadows and slumbering. At least that part of the script will be somewhat familiar to me since I heard him say it.

"Okay," says the man in the black turtleneck sweater, checking the sign-up sheet. "Jacky Hart. You're here for Puck?"

"Yes, sir."

Ms. O'Mara claps.

"This is the girl you told us about?" asks the man in the goatee.

"She's great." Ms. O'Mara shoots me a double thumbs-up while the man in the black turtleneck hands me a sheet of paper.

"Here are your sides," he says.

"Thank you."

Sides are what they call the part of the script they want you to read.

Except my sides aren't the same as the ones Travis Wormowitz just read.

Time for a panic attack.

I'm going to have to give a c-c-cold reading again. And you know how the first one turned out!

CHAPTER 19

I stare at the words.

Okay. The first ones are the ones we heard Wormowitz read when we were spying on him through the basement window.

I can power through those!

"I'll follow you, I'll lead you about a round,
Through bog, through bush, through brake,
through briar."

I look up from the sheet of paper. Ms. O'Mara is nodding. Letting me know I'm doing fine. Encouraging me to keep on going.

I do.

Uh-oh. Here come the words I've never seen before, and a lot of them have an *h* in them, just like my last name, Hart. Which, as you might recall, is the word I couldn't say without stuttering that turned me into Jacky Ha-Ha-Hart.

"'Sometime a h-h-horse I'll be, sometime a h-h-hound.'"

I'm h-h-having a h-h-hard time stumbling through the words, so I improvise a quick gag.

"Ah-oooo!" I howl. "That's my, uh, h-h-hound," I explain.

The adults stare at me. Except Ms. O'Mara. She stares at whatever she's doodling on her notepad.

"'A h-h-hog, a h-h-headless b-b-bear.'" I stop. "Okay, that would be weird, right? A b-b-bear without a h-h-head? Did they have those running around in Shakespeare's day? If so, w-w-wouldn't they just keep b-b-bumping into trees because they couldn't see where they were going? It'd be w-w-worse than W-W-Winnie the P-P-Pooh with his h-h-head stuck in a h-h-honey jar. By the w-w-way, what sort of last name is P-P-Pooh, anyway? A stinky one, if you ask me. And h-h-how about his middle name? 'The.' Wh-wh-what's up with that?"

And speaking of names, what sort of name is Sh-Sh-Shakespeare? Were his ancestors fierce w-w-warriors who shook spears or s-s-something?

Judging from the judges' reaction, my improvised comedy routine isn't exactly a huge hit.

"Miss Hart?" says the guy with the goatee. "Please stick to the script."

"Right. My b-b-bad."

This is going about as badly as the morning announcements. In desperation, I jump to the end of the sides.

"And n-n-neigh, and b-b-bark, and g-g-grunt,
and roar, and b-b-burn,

Like h-h-horse, h-h-hound, h-h-hog, bear, fire, at every t-t-turn.”

For good (or bad) measure, I toss in a whinny, another beagle howl, a pig snort, and a bear growl. I would’ve done fire, too, but I’m not exactly sure how to make a snap-crackle-and-pop noise without a bowl of Rice Krispies.

As my bear growl fades away, the people at the table all glance at each other. All except Ms. O’Mara, who is still staring at her doodles.

“O-kay,” says the guy with the goatee, who I’m starting to think is the director, also known as the one who’ll make the final decision about who plays what part. I’m also pretty sure that, right now, he’s on Team Wormowitz.

“Let’s move on to the other fairies,” says the director. “Kathy? Can you read them in?”

“Sure,” says Ms. O’Mara as the man in the black turtleneck hands sides to Bill, Dan, Jeff, and Meredith.

I guess there are only four other fairies. I start to move off to the side in defeat, but Meredith stops me.

“Um, I’ve changed my mind,” says Meredith.

"I don't really want a speaking role. Here you go, Jacky."

She hands me her sheet of paper.

"Would you be in the chorus?" asks Ms. Sherron. "Because we really want to add some musical interludes to this show. . . ."

"Sure," says Meredith. "I'd rather sing than speak, any day."

Me too, I think. *Especially today.*

CHAPTER 20

Okay," says the director. "Bill, you try Cobweb. Jeff, you'll be Moth."

"I promise not to fly too close to any candles or bug zappers," cracks Jeff.

Everybody laughs. (Something they weren't doing during my recent joke-fest.)

"Dan," says the director, "why don't you try Peaseblossom."

"Is that like a pea plant?" asks Dan. "With a flower?"

"I'm not really sure. . . ."

"No problem. If I get the part, I'll research it like crazy."

"Good attitude." Finally, the director turns to me. "Jacky, you can read Mustardseed."

"Yes, sir."

"Okay," says the director. "Kathy is Titania, the queen of the fairies. She is your fearless leader."

Ms. O'Mara takes her place in the middle of her four fairies.

"Whenever you're ready, Kath," says the director. She reads us into the scene.

"I'll give thee fairies to attend on thee,
And they shall fetch thee jewels from the deep,
And sing while thou on pressed flowers dost
sleep . . ."

I'm picturing that in my head. Pressed flowers sound like a pretty flat pillow. I'd rather have them unpressed and fluffy if I'm going to sleep on them. And what if you're allergic to pollen? You're gonna wake up sneezing, with snot all over yourself.

"'Peaseblossom!'" cries Ms. O'Mara. "'Cobweb! Moth! and Mustardseed!'"

That's our big cue.

Dan goes first. "'Ready!'"

"'And I,'" says Bill as Cobweb.

Jeff, our Moth, is next. "'And I.'"

I bring up the rear as Mustardseed. "'And I!'"

No stuttering. Maybe because Jeff and Bill already said the exact same line I say.

"Do we read this next part?" asks Jeff. "Where it says 'All'?"

"Yes," says the director. "That means all of you; all the fairies."

We nod. Look at each other.

"On three," says Bill. "One, two, three . . ."

"'Where shall we go?'" the four of us say together.

"Great," says the director, because that's all the lines for the fairy auditions. Fairies are teeny, tiny mythical creatures. Apparently, they're even teenier and tinier parts in *A Midsummer Night's Dream*. If I land the role of Mustardseed, I think I already memorized all of my lines.

"Great work, guys," says Ms. O'Mara. "But in the

show, we can't do the countdown thing before you all speak together."

"Got it," says Dan. "Shakespeare didn't write 'one, two, three.' We'll work on some other sort of nonverbal cue for the group lines."

"Thanks for coming in on a Saturday, kids," says the director. "Now we have some tough decisions to make. You all wrote your phone numbers on the sign-up sheet, right?"

We nod.

"Great. We'll let you know either way in a few days. Thanks again for coming in."

"Catch up with you guys later," says Ms. O'Mara. "We have some more actors coming in this afternoon."

"For fairies?" asks Jeff.

"No. Other parts."

"So we have a shot?"

"Yes, Jeff."

"Booyah!"

We head up the stairs. Everybody else is feeling pretty great. We may end up with ridiculously small parts (especially when compared with the juicy roles we've had in our school productions), but we'd be in the big Shakespeare Down the Shore show with Ms. O'Mara and Latoya Sherron!

But, inside, I know I've totally blown my chance to play the part I really want to play.

Puck.

I guess I should've read the script before going to the audition, huh?

CHAPTER 21

After the audition, I go to work at the Balloon Race booth on the boardwalk.

I'm pretty mad at myself. I should've practiced my lines—or even *looked* at them before today. I should've stuck to the script instead of cracking jokes. I should've realized that Shakespeare's lines were better than mine because, hello, he's Shakespeare and I'm Jacky Ha-Ha. Yes, I'm *should*-ing all over myself. Pouting on a stool in a plywood booth surrounded by freaky clowns with balloons growing out of the pointy nozzles in their heads.

"Yo, Jacky?" says Vinnie. "Wake up, why don't you? We've got potential customers here."

The boardwalk, of course, is packed. It's a

Saturday, so we have more day-trippers than usual.

I launch into my usual spiel. It works pretty well. Then, after maybe two hours, I dip into my back pocket where I stuck my sides from the audition and pull out Mr. Shakespeare's words. I'm curious if I can say them without stuttering if I do them in character as a carnival barker.

"Ladies and gentlemen, boys and girls: It's time to neigh and bark and grunt and roar and burn. Step right up and take your turn."

"What the . . ." says Vinnie. "What's all them animal noises got to do with shooting squirt guns at a clown or popping balloons?"

I shrug. "Just trying to shake things up a bit."

My goofy idea works. I fill the firing line with eager squirt gunners. They do funny grunts, growls, squeals, and squawks as they wait for the starting bell to ring.

Vinnie is impressed with the power of my words, words, words.

"Good job, Jacky," he says, stuffing another wad of cash into his money box. "Keep on being goofy. Goofy is good."

I finally head home around seven. Mom and

Sophia have pulled together our standard summer Saturday dinner: hot dogs, baked beans, and canned potato sticks.

"How was work this week, girls?" asks Dad after we've all had dessert.

That's our cue.

Time for all the Hart girls, except Riley and Emma, to add our paychecks to the family piggy bank, which is actually a cookie jar shaped like a pig.

"Mr. Williams gave me a ten-cents-an-hour raise," reports Victoria. "Apparently, every time I'm working the taffy-pulling machine in the front window, business goes up ten percent. It's because I smile. And a smile is happiness you can find right under your nose!"

She (finally) plops her paycheck into the pot.

"I was docked a half day's pay at the Fudgery," Hannah reports glumly. "I didn't think they would deduct the cost of the free samples I sampled."

"That's okay, dear," says Mom.

"How else am I supposed to know what all the different fudge flavors taste like?"

"You'll do better next week," says Dad.

I can tell they feel sort of bad about putting this much of a financial burden on their daughters' shoulders.

"I did okay," reports Sophia, stuffing a roll of cash into the cookie jar. She's waitressing at a sit-down restaurant, so most of her paycheck is actually paper money. "Except some people just aren't very good tippers. Including some people I thought were my friends . . ."

I go last. "Vinnie gave me a bonus. Sales are way up. People seem to like my snappy patter."

"Way to go, Jacky!" says Dad when I add my check and cash bonus to the family's bank account. "You really found a way to put your talents to work."

The way he says "talents," I know he really means my weird and wacky antics. The ones, as a straight-laced cop type, he's never really understood.

"Thank you all," says Mom.

"Definitely," adds Dad. "Thanks to you guys, this summer is going to be a great start to the rest of our lives!"

Victoria applauds. "Bravo! Well said." Hannah, Riley, and Sophia join in.

I fake yet another smile and clap along with my sisters.

How could this summer be a great start to the rest of *my* life?

I know in my heart I won't be playing Puck. That my dream of being an actress or a performer is a big, fat joke. Unless, of course, the only shows I want to do are on the boardwalk with clowns and balloons.

Travis Wormowitz, the star of the high school drama club, is going to wind up a winner this summer.

Me?

I'm well on my way to L-L-Loserville.

CHAPTER 22

Later that night, I take Sandfleas out for a walk.
We head toward the boardwalk.

When I've done shows in the past, my nightly dog walks have been when I work on my lines. So, maybe just to prove to myself that I can, I recite a little Shakespeare to Sandfleas.

"'And neigh, and bark . . .'"

Sandfleas barks. It's one of the tricks I taught her.

"Good girl." I plow ahead with the lines I memorized after dinner, taking my time, saying all the words without a single stumble or stutter. "'And grunt, and roar, and burn, / Like horse, hound, hog, bear, fire, at every turn.'"

GO KARTS
to pee or not to pee...
There is **no** question. I need to find a fire hydrant... **fast**!

Sandfleas wags her tail. I think she likes Shakespeare. Especially when it rolls trippingly off my tongue, which by the way, was the advice Shakespeare gave to a group of actors in his play *Hamlet.* He also told them not to saw the air too much. He wasn't big on exaggerated arm gestures. Or lumberjacks, I guess.

"Guess I should've looked at Puck's lines before the audition, huh?" I say to Sandfleas.

She yaps in agreement.

"Lesson learned. If I ever go on another audition, no matter the role, I go in prepared."

(And you know what, ladies? I always do. "Be prepared" is my official motto. I'm like the Boy Scouts.)

I look off to the horizon and see the silhouette of the Ferris wheel, black against the twinkling night sky. It's the same one I climbed to make a solemn vow and howl at the moon, as you might recall.

I'm thinking about climbing it again so I can make another solemn vow: If I ever get another shot to do what I love to do more than anything in the world, I will not waste it. The acting bug has bitten me hard. It's up to me to be disciplined enough to take my talent to the next level, which isn't up at the top of a Ferris wheel anymore.

"You want to climb it?" asks a voice behind me.

It's Bob.

"'Cause I'm down for anything."

"Not tonight," I tell him, tugging on Sandfleas' leash. "I don't think my dog would approve. I'd have to drag her along like a floppy puppet on a string."

"I could hold your dog for you if you'd rather climb solo."

"Thanks for the offer, Bob. But I made a solemn vow that I wouldn't climb any more Ferris wheels."

"When'd you do that?"

"The last time I climbed the Ferris wheel. Way up at the top there. It's a good spot for solemn vowing."

Bob nods. "I'm totally down with that, too."

"Hey, Bob?"

"Yeah?"

"Can I ask you a question?"

"Sure."

I hesitate, then plow ahead. "Why are you suddenly acting like a decent human being?"

He shrugs. "Not sure. Just thought, you know, I'd

give it a whirl. Try something different. Well, I better bounce. Have a nice dog walk, Jacky. I'm outtie!"

Bob strolls away. For half a second, I think about following him. Sandfleas sniffs the air to let me know the boy would be easy to track. His scent (or Calvin Klein's) is on the breeze.

But then I hear a giggle.

From underneath the boardwalk.

It's a giggle I recognize.

My sister Sophia!

CHAPTER 23

Have you ever heard that song "Under the Boardwalk," by the Drifters?

The lyrics paint a pretty picture:

(Under the boardwalk) people walking above
(Under the boardwalk) we'll be falling in love

Trust me, the real deal is nowhere near as romantic. There's a lot of gross stuff down there. We're talking slimy seaweed, grungy rodent poop, and rusty soda cans—not to mention discarded slices of pizza. From last year.

Streaks of moonlight are filtering through the boards. I can see that Sophia is with a boy. A boy I don't recognize. For sure it isn't Mike Guadagno, this prepster Sophia and Hannah both had a mega crush on last fall. Sophia has already fallen "madly, deeply" in love with six other boys since then. Meanwhile, Hannah is still using her employee discount to buy boxes of peanut butter fudge for Mike G.

The guy Sophia's flirting with tonight is tall and lanky with a thick head of wavy hair. He kind of reminds me of John Stamos, the handsome hunk who plays Jesse Katsopolis on the TV show *Full House*. He's wearing black jeans and a black T-shirt that match his awesome black hair.

The guy might be a tourist. Someone visiting Seaside Heights for a week or two with his family. Or he could just be a local I haven't met yet. Sophia and the boy aren't kissing or anything yucky like that, otherwise Sandfleas and I would both be tossing up our cookies (or dog biscuits). The guy's just looking totally chill, leaning up against a pole with his hair perfectly framing his face. Sophia, on the other hand, is giggling and working the toe of her tennis shoe into the sand.

"So you'll be here all summer?" she asks.

"Yeah. I'm hangin' at my aunt's crib. She's wicked dank."

"Huh?"

"Means she's awesome."

"Wow. You really are from Philly. You know all the slang we never hear around here."

"Yeah," says the guy. "I'm looking forward to learning more about Seaside Heights." He takes a step toward Sophia. "Seeing *all* the beautiful sights . . . including you."

Urp. Barf alert.

Sandfleas grumbles out a low, throaty growl.

It inspires me.

I howl. The same werewolf-under-a-full-moon howl I did at the top of the Ferris wheel, only this howl echoes a lot more, bouncing around underneath the boardwalk. It's like I'm yodeling in the Alps, which I think is the number one tourist thing to do in Switzerland.

"AH-WOOOO-OOO-OOO-OOOO-OOO . . ."

The boy looks over and probably sees a silhouette of a snarling dog and a howling crazy girl with her hands cupped over her mouth.

"Uh, catch you later, Olivia," the boy says before he takes off running.

"Sophia!" my sister calls after him. "My name is Sophia."

"My bad," says the boy, who is already fifty feet away.

Sophia twirls around so she has a better angle to glare at me.

"Sandfleas? Is that you? Jacqueline?!?"

I do a finger-wiggle wave. Sandfleas waggles her tail.

Sophia kicks at the sand. "Schuyler was going to be my one true love."

For this week, anyway, I think.

"Why do you have to ruin everything for everybody else, Jacky? Why?"

My big sister stomps away, sobbing dramatically.

Yeah. I sometimes have that effect on people. Sometimes, even on myself.

CHAPTER 24

The next day, I apologize to Sophia at breakfast.

"I didn't mean to, you know, ruin your date," I tell her.

"I wasn't on a date last night, Jacky. I was right here at home, in my room. Working on my summer reading list. *The Great Gatsby* is, um, great. Especially if you like Gatsbys."

Did I mention that Mom is in the kitchen, wolfing down a quick cup of coffee and a doughnut before heading off to cop school? (I'm wondering if Comparative Doughnuts 101 is a class they teach at the police academy, since cops love doughnuts so much.)

“Be good, guys,” Mom says as she packs up her stuff.

“Or you’ll arrest us, right?” I joke.

“Can’t,” she jokes back. “Have to ace the course first!”

She walks out the door. I slurp down a bowl of Lucky Charms (they’re magically delicious) and head off to work on the boardwalk. Sophia sticks out her tongue at me from the front window. All is not forgiven.

At the Balloon Race booth, business is pretty slow before noon. There have only been three races so far, and the biggest prize anyone won was a huge neon-green stuffed snake.

So I spend my downtime reading *A Midsummer Night’s Dream,* which I found on the bookshelf in the room Sydney used to share with Sophia and Victoria. There’s a reason my oldest sister got into Princeton on a full-ride scholarship. The girl was always reading everything—especially stuff that “challenged her,” like Shakespeare, Charles Dickens, Mark Twain, and Jane Austen. She also has an incredible collection of comic books—mostly Wonder Woman. I think she’s her role model.

I'm already up to act 3, scene 2 of *MSND* when I come to this line that Puck says right before he exits the stage:

I go, I go; look how I go,
Swifter than arrow from the Tartar's bow.

I'm not sure what a Tartar is. They're probably the people who invented tartar sauce.

So maybe the Tartars were also the people who invented the Filet-O-Fish sandwich at Mickey Dee's.

I make a note in the margins to look the word up. Because if I ever get another chance to play Puck, I want to make sure I know what all the words mean.

Later at work, I try to drum up my first crowd of squirt gun shooters with a semi-Shakespearean chant.

"Hey ho, hey ho; look how you go. Squirt the gun, make the balloon blow."

"I'll give it a shot," says Bob, ambling up to the front of the booth.

I'm starting to wonder if he's stalking me. Also, he's done something very strange with his hair. I think he's combed it.

"Okay, we have one shooter," I say into my microphone. "But we need two to play. Who's ready to make a clown pay?"

"Me," says Bill, who also just mysteriously appears. He takes the squirt gun right next to Bob.

"Um, aren't you supposed to be at work?" I ask him.

"I'm on break." He bobs his head toward, well, Bob. "Is this big galoot bothering you?"

Yes, I want to say. *But not in the usual way.* He's kind of making my stomach do weird somersaults and backflips. Why? I have no idea.

"What's a galoot?" asks Bob, narrowing his eyes at Bill.

"Look in the mirror," says Bill. "You'll see."

"Oh, yeah?"

"Yeah."

Bob flexes his squirt gun trigger finger. "Fine. Game on, Billy Boy."

Bill crouches down to line up his clown mouth shot. "Bring it, Bobbo. Bring it."

Wow. If I didn't know better, I'd say these two boys were challenging each other to a duel . . . over me.

CHAPTER 25

The bell rings.

A needle-thin jet of water blasts out of both squirt guns to hit the clown targets. With their fingers on the triggers, Bob and Bill use just about every other part of their bodies to bump and nudge each other.

They're both doing everything they can to throw off the other guy's aim and win . . . me?

I feel like Sophia must feel on a regular basis. It's pretty cool to have two guys fighting over you.

"Hey, hey, hey," says Vinnie when Bob gives Bill a good butt bump and Bill pushes back with a left elbow jab to Bob's shooting arm. "That's against the rules, youse two."

“All’s fair in love and war!” shouts Bill.

“Is that more stupid stuff from Shakespeare?” demands Bob.

“No! That one’s from me!” cries Bill as his balloon pops a half second before Bob’s. “We have a winner! Me!”

I have never seen Bill look so excited or, you know, slightly crazed.

Bob slumps his shoulders. “Best two out of three?” he asks.

“No thanks,” says Bill. “I prefer one and done!”

Defeated, Bob slides his squirt gun back into its metal bracket.

“See you ’round, Jacky.”

“Yeah,” I say. “Catch you later, Bob.”

Bob slouches off, hands stuffed deep inside his pockets. Vinnie gives Bill a fuzzy pink poodle key chain—the cheapest prize in the booth.

“Here youse go, kid. Play another game, trade up to a prize that ain’t so lame.”

“No thank you,” Bill tells Vinnie. Then he turns to me. “What did that mean?”

“That if you played again you could win a better prize.”

"I meant that thing with Bob. 'Catch you later'? Come on, Jacky. That's Bubblebutt we're talking about. Bubble. Butt."

"His name is Bob."

"So are you and he dating or something?"

"Why? Are you jealous or something?"

Wow. Boy-girl stuff is difficult. Especially for a girl who, two weeks ago, didn't really think about boys all that much. They were just friends. Now does one have to become my boyfriend? Is that a rule?

Bill and I might've discussed it further, but Vinnie is standing right there, giving me his version of Mom's Look.

"Jacky?" he says. "This big-spender friend of yours here says he's one and done. So you need to bid him adieu, like your pal Shakespeare says. I need youse to drum up a little more business here. Otherwise, I'm not going to have enough pesos in my pockets to buy a Pepsi with my pizza!"

I look at Bill.

He looks at me.

"Later." We both say it at the same time.

And then we both go back to working our summer jobs. I throw myself into my carnival barker banter with renewed vigor. I work in some new clown jokes I found in Emma's *Circus Jokes and Riddles* book.

"My parents hired a clown for my birthday party once. It was terrible. The guy was such a Bozo. Why does the blue clown down there look so sad? Because the last shooter broke his funny bone. I wouldn't want to take over the clown's job, though. Those are big shoes to fill."

By three o'clock, I have a whole mob waiting to take their shot at the crazy clowns. They're lined up four deep behind all eight squirt guns. Vinnie is raking in boatloads of cash.

Two new players push their way to the front of the crowd.

Two cops.

My dad and his partner, Flattop.

CHAPTER 26

My dad still looks like the most handsome boy on the beach, as he was called in his younger days, even decked out in his police-blue pants, sky-blue polo shirt, and navy-blue cop cap.

Flattop, of course, has a much more official-looking uniform. He also has a badge and a holstered pistol.

I can't resist making Dad and his boss the stars of my improvised balloon booth show.

"Well, well, well," I say into my microphone. "Here come two real straight shooters, ladies and gentlemen. Seaside Heights' Finest. Quick Draw McGraw and his partner Mega Mighty Mac Hart. Which one of these two boys in blue will be crowned Top Cop here at the balloon pop?"

Dad smiles.

"What do you say, Tom?" Dad says to his senior partner. "Want to give it a try?"

"What?" says the cop with the gray bristle-brush hair. "You think you can outshoot me, rookie?"

Dad shrugs. "I don't get paid to think, sir. But I'm pretty decent with a squirt gun. My daughters taught me. . . ."

"Let's do this thing," says his senior partner, Tom, grabbing a gun.

Seeing Dad and Tom assuming their firing stances, jockeying for any slight advantage, reminds me of Bob and Bill doing the same thing. I guess boys never really grow up even when they become men.

The spectacle of two cops in a water pistol shoot-out makes my already-swollen crowd grow even larger. Vinnie's money box is bulging with cash. He's practically drooling. Guys are paying double to shoot it out against the two police officers.

I gulp a little.

I sure hope Dad wins. If he doesn't, I'm afraid several hundred people are going to laugh at him.

When all the firing slots are filled, Vinnie rings the bell. The water whooshes through the guns. The tin targets are blasted with sizzling water streams. The balloons start inflating.

I call the play-by-play.

"Officer Tom takes an early lead. But, look out, Mac Hart is hitting the dead center of his clown's bull's-eye. He's throwing his water straight down the middle and over the plate—just like he did when he played baseball for the Yankees."

Dad laughs but keeps his aim steady.

"Sure, it was the minor-league Oneonta Yankees, but Mac Hart knows how to fire one into the catcher's mitt or the clown's mouth."

I swing into the kind of catcher chatter I used to do behind the plate when I played on an otherwise-all-boys Little League team (back when summer vacation didn't mean I had to have a job and serious responsibilities).

"Hey, squirt gunner can't squirt. Hey, balloon, balloon. Pop!"

BANG!

Dad's balloon bursts first. The crowd roars. I do a happy dance like Snoopy did in *You're a Good Man, Charlie Brown.*

Dad's prize, besides bragging rights, of course, is pretty awesome. Vinnie is extremely generous. He hands Dad a teddy bear decked out in a New York Yankees uniform. That's a level-ten prize—and he's definitely earned it!

"I'll beat you next time," says his new buddy Tom, slapping Dad on the back and laughing.

"Yes, sir," says Dad. "I'm sure you will."

"Especially if you want to win that full-time job after Labor Day," says Tom.

Dad smiles and hands the giant stuffed bear back to me. "Can you take it home for me, Jacky?" he asks. "I can't really walk the beat with a teddy bear tucked under my arm. No matter how awesome he looks."

Dad and I are actually having a pretty sweet moment.

But then he has to go and spoil it all by saying what I've already started thinking.

You'll make a great cop, Dad.
And you already make a great daughter, Jacky.

"You're really good at this, Jacky. Hey, maybe this is what you should do with your, you know, flair for showbiz. When you grow up, you could run your own booth, right here on the boardwalk. Wouldn't that be great?"

"Yes, sir," I say, even though, to tell the truth, in 1991 my dreams are a little bigger than being a carnival barker in Seaside Heights.

About an hour after Dad leaves the booth, Ms. O'Mara comes along.

And the news she has to share makes me think that Dad is right.

A balloon-pop booth might be as far as I'll ever make it in showbiz.

CHAPTER 27

Travis Wormowitz is going to be our Puck," Ms. O'Mara tells me. "He handled the language a little better."

I nod. It's true.

If the part went to the actor who *mangled* the language best, I would've been a shoo-in.

"Travis was better prepared than me," I say.

"Yes, Jacky, he was," says Ms. O'Mara, because she's super-honest that way and doesn't sugarcoat stuff.

I'm on my break from the booth. We're both sipping Cokes out of waxy cups.

Was this the big, colossal mistake I made that

summer? (Blowing the Puck audition, not sipping Coke out of a waxy cup.)

Well, it was a big one, girls. No doubt about it.

But, believe it or not, that wasn't the biggest blunder I made that particular summer. This was *not* my colossal failure—even though, at the time, it sure felt like it.

"We'd still love for you to be in the show," says Ms. O'Mara.

"As one of the fairies?"

She nods. "We'd also like you to understudy the part of Puck."

"Understudy? What's that? Do I have to crawl under Travis and study math or something?"

"No, Jacky," Ms. O'Mara laughs. "As the understudy, you would learn the role of Puck—all the lines, all the staging—so you'd be able to replace Travis if, for whatever reason, he couldn't go on."

"You mean like if someone accidentally on purpose tripped him while he was Rollerblading and he went flying off the boardwalk, flipped over the railing, and sailed down to the beach, where he hit a concrete bench and twisted his ankle so badly he ended up in the hospital annoying all the nurses?"

Now it's Ms. O'Mara's turn to give me Mom's patented arched-eyebrow look. (It's like all grown-ups share the same scowl.)

"Jacky?" she says.

"Kidding," I say, throwing up both hands.

"It'll be a great learning experience," Ms. O'Mara tells me. "When you memorize words . . ."

"I don't have as much trouble saying them," I finish for her.

"Exactly."

Then I start thinking about what Dad said. I

am really good at my job in the booth. It may not be Shakespeare, but it's fun. I make people laugh. I make money. I help Mom and Dad achieve their dreams.

But it's a summer job, and summer lasts only three months. What am I supposed to do the other nine months of the year? Repair punctured balloons for the coming season? Learn more clown jokes? Clean out squirt gun nozzles with bent safety pins?

And do I really want to be a big fish in a little pond all my life?

"Which fairy do you guys want me to play?" I ask.

"Mustardseed."

"That's the one who only has one line. 'And I,' right?"

"She has four other lines," says Ms. O'Mara. "'Hail.' 'Mustardseed.' 'Ready.' And 'What's your will?'"

"Five lines?"

"Plus all the group lines."

I nod. It isn't very much, but it's what I deserve, considering I didn't prepare for the audition.

"It'll give you more time to memorize the Puck speeches," says Ms. O'Mara.

I can tell she really wants me to do this. I also have a feeling Dad (and probably Mom) really won't want me to. It might interfere with the long-term boardwalk barker career plans they have for me.

"When's the first rehearsal?" I ask.

"Tomorrow. The same church. The same basement."

I think about it for another half second and then give the only answer Jacky Ha-Ha possibly could:

"I'll see you there, Ms. O'Mara."

CHAPTER 28

Because I don't like it when anybody does something sneaky without telling me (like studying to be a cop without informing his children), I tell Mom and Dad that I got a "teeny, tiny part" in the Shakespeare Down the Shore show.

"Will it interfere with your work schedule?" asks Dad.

"No. This part is so small, I'll probably only have to go to one rehearsal. Maybe one and a half."

Mom tells me to "have fun with it."

"But don't neglect your other responsibilities," adds Dad.

"Yeah," says Riley, who doesn't want to wind up

getting stuck on permanent Emma-watching duty.

The first rehearsal is after work. I meet Bill at the T-Shirt Hut so we can walk over to the church together. We need to talk.

"Sorry about saying that stuff about you being jealous," I tell him.

"No. I'm sorry."

"Bob is turning into a decent human being," I tell Bill. "I think we should encourage that."

"Definitely," says Bill. "The more decent human beings, the better." He pauses. "So does this mean we can't call him Bubblebutt anymore?"

"Not if we want to be, you know, decent human beings."

Bill nods. "What about Ringworm?"

I think about that for a second. "I guess it's okay for now. I don't even know his real name."

"Cool."

"Pals?" I say, holding out my hand.

"Pals," says Bill, taking it.

We shake. But Bill doesn't let go of my hand exactly when he should, if you know what I mean. He lingers. I don't mind. Lingering feels good. You know what else feels good? Being able to just talk to him.

The church basement rehearsal hall is buzzing with electricity, and not just because that's where the circuit breaker box is located. Everyone is super-excited about our first read-through of the script.

I still get that tingly feeling every time I start a show. The sense that anything is possible. That adventure awaits. And that my fellow travelers are just as jazzed as I am to be making the trip into the unknown together.

Dan, Meredith, and Jeff come into the basement a few minutes after Bill and me.

We all say hello to Latoya Sherron and she says hello to us, just like she weren't a big star, which, of course, she totally is. Riley has cartoons of her and MC Hammer on her lunch box (which used to be *my* lunch box).

Ms. O'Mara introduces us to Oliver and Quinn Reinhardt. They're twins, even though they don't look exactly alike. Oliver will be playing Lysander, one of the young lovers in *A Midsummer Night's Dream*. His brother, Quinn, is playing Demetrius.

"Shakespeare was big on twins and mistaken identities," says Quinn.

"But not in *Dream,*" says Oliver. "In this play, my character, Lysander, loves Hermia and she loves Lysander."

"But," says Quinn, "my character, Demetrius, used to love Helena, but now he loves Hermia, too. Hermia's dad thinks I'm a better match for his daughter than Lysander, so he gets the duke of Athens to force Hermia to marry me."

"Even though Hermia would much rather marry me," says Oliver.

"And Helena still has the hots for me," says Quinn.

We all just stand there and nod. Shakespeare is more complicated than a soap opera that's been on TV since forever.

"A lot of Shakespeare's plays start with a father

trying to block his daughter's true love or passion," explains Ms. O'Mara.

Hmm, I think. *Sounds vaguely familiar.*

"Okay, is everybody here?" asks the guy with the goatee. He is, indeed, our director. His name is Scott.

"We're still missing Travis Wormowitz," reports Ms. O'Mara.

"Right," says Scott. "Our Puck . . ."

"Sorry I'm late!" booms Travis, appearing, right on cue, at the top of the staircase. He does some dainty fairy skips down the steps, making a grand, dramatic entrance, while reciting Puck's final speech from the play.

I could have said the lines with Travis because I've memorized them. It's what we understudies do.

We just don't always get a chance to say them out loud.

If we shadows have offended, think but this and all is mended—that you have but slumber'd here while these visions did appear.... And I am definitely a Vision.

And I definitely want to SLUMBER....

CHAPTER 29

There's a saying in the theater: There are no small parts, only small actors.

So when it comes time for us to read our fairy scenes with the full cast, I give my five Mustardseed lines everything I have. No way do I want to let my cast down. Even if I had only one line instead of five, I would say it as if the whole show depended on me and that one sentence.

I think it was that first rehearsal of my first Shakespeare show down in that musty church basement that made me decide, once and for all, that I wanted to be a professional performer for the rest of my life—no matter what. As the late, great Ethel Merman once sang, "There's no business like show business like no business I know."

The song is correct. And I just had to be a part of that big, crazy showbiz world.

But Travis Wormowitz? I think he wants to be a star. The kind that throws hissy fits and ends up in gossip magazines, usually after punching a photographer.

"Excuse me," he huffs during our first read-through of the whole play. "But what is a Tartar's bow? Is that like something fairies wear in their hair?"

I raise my hand.

"What?" snaps Travis.

"Um, according to what I found at the library, a Tartar's bow was a recurve bow that was shorter than most archery bows."

What ho! Check out my Tartar bow! No, I am not aiming it at Travis....

"It was also made out of horn and other seriously stiff material," I continue, "so a Tartar's bow had more power than a regular bow. More power meant faster arrows. So Puck is basically saying he'll be really, really, *really* speedy."

Everybody laughs. Except Travis Wormowitz, of course.

"Thank you, Jacky Ha-Ha," he snarls through a fake smile. "That is what they call you at school, isn't it?"

"Because she's funny," says Bill, defending me.

"Hysterical," sneers Travis. "Tell you what, Jacky: Since your part is so teensy tiny in this show, you can do *all* my homework for me."

"Jacky is just doing her job like a pro," says Scott, the director. "After all, she is understudying the role of Puck."

"What? Why?"

"For the same reason I'm understudying Latoya's part," says Ms. O'Mara. "The show must go on, even if one of our leads can't."

"Well, if you play her part, who plays yours?" Travis asks Ms. O'Mara.

"*My* understudy."

He rolls his eyes. The guy is extremely babyish. "It seems sort of stupid. All these people learning all these different parts. Everybody just don't get sick, okay?" He turns to me. "I know I won't. I'm healthy as a horse. A thoroughbred. The kind that wins races and becomes super-famous, like Seattle Slew!"

"Who's Seattle Stu?" cracks Jeff. "Never heard of the guy."

The room laughs.

"Okay, everybody," says Scott. "Let's circle back to Shakespeare. Travis, pick it up with your line again, please."

Travis recites the Puck speech without stopping to ask any more questions about what words mean. He sounds very singsongy, like he did at his audition. But he also sounds like he doesn't really know what he's saying. It's all just words, words, words to him.

And I might not be the only one thinking that way.

Maybe it's just my overactive imagination, but Scott, Ms. O'Mara, Ms. Sherron—even the Reinhardt twins—are kind of giving Travis a skeptical stink eye!

CHAPTER 30

At the end of the rehearsal, a moody dude with shaggy hair lopes down the steps into the basement with his hands stuffed into the front pockets of his hoodie.

It's Schuyler! The boy Sophia was gaga over underneath the boardwalk. I recognize his wavy John Stamos hairdo.

"Hey, Aunt Kathy," he says to Ms. O'Mara.

"Hey, Schuyler," says Ms. O'Mara.

She wraps her arms around him in a big hug. Instead of hugging back, he keeps his hands tucked inside his pockets.

"Did you have fun today?" Ms. O'Mara asks.

He shrugs.

"What'd you do?"

"Nothin'."

O-kay. The boy is definitely moody and melancholy. His skin is kind of pale and pasty, too. I suspect he might live in a cave. Too bad Shakespeare Down the Shore isn't doing *Hamlet* this summer. Schuyler would be perfect for the title role of the gloomy prince.

"You guys?" says Ms. O'Mara. "This is my nephew, Schuyler."

"Hey, man," says Jeff, reaching out to give Schuyler a cool-dude handgrip. "'Sup?"

(Yes, that's how we said "What's up?" in 1991.)

"Hey," says Schuyler, halfheartedly returning Jeff's flashy handgrip. "Just so you know, bro—I'm in high school. I don't hang out with middle school nerds."

"Schuyler?" says Ms. O'Mara, shaking her head.

"That's cool," says Dan. "I won't hang out with nerds like me when I'm in high school, either."

Schuyler grins. Slightly. "Sorry, bro. No disrespect."

"None taken," says Bill.

"I'm in high school," says Travis. "You can hang with me. Maybe. But not right now. I need to see my stylist. Gonna get a man-perm so I can play Puck with curly hair."

Travis bows and makes a flashy exit up the stairs, skipping up two, down one, up two the whole way.

When Travis is gone, Schuyler asks, "How old is that doofus?"

"Sixteen," says Ms. O'Mara. "Just like you."

"Wow," I say. "You're ancient."

"He's only four years older than us, Jacky," says Meredith.

"Right. *Four* years. One-third of our entire lives. Do the math, Meredith."

"No thanks. School's out."

"You're right. But sixteen means he's still two years younger than my big sister Sophia."

Schuyler nods, but I can tell he has no idea who Sophia is and why I'm talking about her.

"That's cool," is all he says.

"Schuyler's going to be on the tech crew," says Ms. O'Mara.

"Awesome," says Jeff. "Have you checked out the venue yet?"

"Huh?" says Schuyler.

"The stage. It's the same one they use for the Battle of the Bands."

"It's right on the beach," I add.

"Let's go have a look," suggests Dan.

"Yes," says Meredith. "Let's go see where we're going to be rock stars!"

Jeff looks a little sheepish. "Um, I thought we were going to be, you know . . . fairies."

"Rock star fairies!" I say, doing my best heavy metal arm pump. "Let's hit the beach."

So we take Schuyler down to the Seaside Heights Band Shell—an outdoor amphitheater with a stage built out of risers. There's no ceiling, so the whole show will take place under the stars. It is awesome. It is my favorite place to be in the whole world.

A stage!

Hey, you guys, maybe next year the Shakespeare company can do Annie, because her dog's name is Sandy. Get it? Sandy? We're on a beach....
We got it, Jeff.
But how do we get rid of it?

CHAPTER 31

The audience usually brings beach chairs or just sits on blankets," I tell Schuyler as we check out the stage. "Last summer, I actually saw the Drifters, Gary U.S. Bonds, and Southside Johnny—all right here."

"I might've been wrong about you middle school nerds," says Schuyler, who seems to be loosening up a little. "You guys are okay."

"Yes, we are," says Meredith. "We are also extremely phat."

(Trust me, girls, *phat* meant "cool," not "chubby," back in the '90s.)

"And of course," I tell Schuyler, "the stage is conveniently located right next to the boardwalk. In case, you know, you want to hang out under there with my sister again."

"Huh?"

"Sophia. Or, you know, Olivia. I think that's what you called her after Sandfleas growled and chased you away. . . ."

I can tell from his eyes that a lightbulb just flipped on inside his brain. "You were the girl with the dog."

"Yep. Still am."

"Well, aren't I just the rankest compound of villainous smell that ever offended nostril."

Now it's my turn to be confused. "Huh?"

"It's a Shakespearean insult. Aunt Kathy has been teaching me a bunch of them."

When he's done cracking me up with all the Shakespearean insults he's memorized, Schuyler asks if there's "anything fun to do around here."

"Are you kidding?" I tell him. "You see that pier there? It's called the *Funtown* Pier. You can't get more fun than that. Come on. How about we go over to the boardwalk and play a few games?"

"Cool."

"So you guys—who's up for a quick game of Ringtoss?"

"It's rigged," groans Bill.

"So is the baseball game," says Jeff.

"And the basketball hoops," says Dan.

"They're not rigged," I say with a sly smile. "You just have to know how to beat 'em."

"And you do?" asks Schuyler.

I nod. "At least the ringtoss."

It's time for Jacky Ha-Ha to show off her special skills and boardwalk superpowers.

The Ringtoss booth is conveniently located directly across from my Balloon Race stand. That means I've spent several hours' worth of fifteen-minute breaks learning how to beat the bottles. To win, you have to land your rubber ring on the neck of a glass bottle crowded into a battalion of bottles all lined up in tight and tidy rows.

Whoever drank all those sodas
probably has more gas in them
than the blimp.
GOOD YEAR

"Aim for a close bottle," I tell everybody. "That way, your ring won't get knocked off course." I crouch down. "Try to make sure your ring is on the same plane as the bottle tops before you fling it."

"Whoa," says Jeff. "Listen to Ms. Geometry."

I ignore him. We have to do that a lot with Jeff Cohen.

"Snap your wrist as you fling the ring, like you're throwin' a Frisbee, to get as much spin as possible. It's easier to land on the target cleanly if you're kind of hovering over it like a UFO. You want it to drop straight down to minimize the bounce factor."

I toss my ring. It lands on a bottle.

"Woo-hoo!" shouts Dan.

"Jack-ee, Jack-ee," chants Bill.

"My girl is the bomb," says Meredith.

Schuyler laughs. "This is so cool." He goes to grab a ring.

"Sorry," says the guy running the booth. "We're closed for inventory."

He grabs the bucket of rubber rings.

"What?" I say. "Inventory?"

"Yeah. I gotta count the rings. So do me a favor, little lady. Go back to your boss's booth and ruin *his* day!"

"Fine. After you give me my prize."

"Here," he says, handing me a slip of paper. "It's a coupon. Ten percent off at Willy B. Williams's Taffy Shoppe. Enjoy."

"Huh. That's where my sister Victoria works. Who else is hungry for chewy tubes of gooey sugar?"

Everybody's hands shoot up.

"So let's go see Victoria. And please—nobody call her Vickie. She'll go nutso."

Little did I know that our trip to the Taffy Shoppe would totally change my big sister's life. Forever!

CHAPTER 32

When the six of us stroll into Willy B. Williams's Taffy Shoppe, we see Victoria busily arranging the different colored and striped taffy pieces in their bins.

And since she knows everything about everything, she's also boring a tourist family out of their gourds. As she organizes and reorganizes, she gives them an unwanted history lesson, occasionally gesturing with a fistful of candy.

"Saltwater taffy isn't made with salt water from the ocean like you'd think," she explains. "So how did it get the misleading name? you're probably wondering."

"Um, no," says the dad. "Not really."

Victoria remains oblivious. "Allow me to explain. In 1883, a big storm hit Atlantic City. The waves washed over the boardwalk and flooded all sorts of shops, including a candy store. When a young girl came in after the storm, hoping to buy taffy, the owner looked at his soggy merchandise and said, 'All I have is saltwater taffy.' The little girl didn't get the joke. She just bought the saltwater taffy. The store owner thought it was a catchy name. So it just sort of stuck. The same way taffy sticks to your teeth . . ."

Jeff Cohen's eyes go wide as Victoria explains the history of the shoppe. His jaw drops. "Wow. That girl is *soooo* smart."

"That's Victoria," I tell him. "She's my sister."

"Really? She's so much prettier. . . ."

I want to slug Jeff in the arm, but I can tell: He's been hit by an arrow from Cupid's bow, which is even stronger than that one made by a Tartar.

If Jeff's heart were a big red balloon, and Victoria's gaze were a squirt gun, it'd probably be popping right about now.

I think I'm in LOVE!
To what do I attribute this sudden increase in my breathing and heart rates as my palms begin to sweat?
CHOCOLA
Black choco
Chocolate
3 Layers caramels
Vanilla
Bit-O-Honey
Taffy

Jeff actually swaggers forward.

"So, Victoria, do you guys sell Laffy Taffy?"

"Um, no. Just our own."

"No problemo. You don't need Laffy Taffy. Because I've memorized all the best jokes from their wrappers."

"Is that so?" giggles Victoria, something I've never heard her do before. She's also twisting her hair around a finger. Will wonders never cease?

Bill, Dan, and Meredith are rolling their eyes. We've all heard Jeff recite Laffy Taffy jokes before. He swears the crinkly wrappers are the best joke book ever written.

"Where does the general put his armies?" he asks.

"I don't know," says Victoria.

"In his sleevies! What are the strongest days of the week?"

Victoria shrugs.

"Saturday and Sunday," Jeff tells her. "Every other day is a weekday. What did the finger say to the thumb?"

"I dunno."

"I'm in glove with you."

Victoria blushes.

"Me too," she gasps.

"Huh?" says Jeff.

"I, uh, I'm in 'glove' with Laffy Taffy jokes, too."

Yes, the romantic sparks are definitely sizzling between Victoria and Jeff—even though she's two years older than him. I guess age doesn't really matter when you have laughter and taffy and goo-goo eyes.

While we're all staring at Victoria and Jeff's love scene in the Taffy Shoppe, which could've been written by Shakespeare if, you know, he liked corny jokes, I notice something out of the corner of my eye.

Schuyler.

He's grabbing a fistful of taffy from the nearest bin and stuffing it into his pocket.

He's shoplifting!

CHAPTER 33

Our eyes meet.

Schuyler winks.

I give him Mom's Look. It says, in no uncertain terms, *Put. It. Back!*

Stealing is wrong. Plus, I don't want Victoria getting blamed for the theft because she was too busy falling in love with Jeff Cohen to notice it.

Schuyler gives me another cocky wink.

This time, I don't just do the Look. I mouth out the words: "Put. It. Back."

Now he gives me a look like I'm some kind of a wimp. But he *does* put the wax-paper-wrapped tubes back where he found them.

"Ewww, gross," says a kid, watching Schuyler

pull gummy candy out of his pocket. "That taffy is all warm and squishy now."

Warm taffy
Just like STRINGY BUBBLEGUM on the bottom of your tennis shoe.
Delish.

Victoria snaps out of her love trance.

"No put-backs," she says. "You touch it, you bought it."

I scoop the taffy Schuyler just dumped back into the bin into a clear plastic bag.

"My treat!" I say.

And that's how I spent the allowance part of my salary that week. Why? Because I'm not big on confrontations. I'm more of a laugh-and-leave-it-alone kind of gal. Or at least I was back in 1991.

"Let's go, you guys," I say. "Victoria needs to take care of her other customers."

"It's true," she says, snapping back to her normal self. "Customer service is a hallmark of Willy B. Williams's Taffy Shoppe. Like Mr. Williams always says, 'Good service is good business!'"

"I know *I'll* be back," says Jeff. "I love the service in this shop. No, I *lurve* it, which is even better than love. . . ."

"Come on, you guys. . . ."

I nudge everybody out the door and pass around the taffy I bought because Schuyler was trying to steal it.

"So, Jacky," says Jeff. "Is your sister dating anybody?"

"Victoria? Nope. In fact, I don't think she's ever been on a date. . . ."

"Awesome! That means she won't have any boys to compare me to. I have a shot! Woo-hoo! Catch you guys later. I have to get moo-ving. I'm late for work."

Later, after everybody else has peeled off and headed to their jobs or homes, Schuyler and I are alone on the boardwalk.

"I was just goofing around," he tells me.

"No," I say. "You were shoplifting."

"You're right," he says. "I am a sodden-witted lord

that hath no more brain than I have in mine elbows."

"Shakespeare?"

"Sort of. I, you know, changed it around a little."

I shake my head. "See you tomorrow, Schuyler."

"'Tomorrow, and tomorrow, and tomorrow, / Creeps in this petty pace from day to day. . . .'"

"What's that from?"

"*Macbeth*. Shakespeare wrote that one, too. Catch you later, kid. I've got to bounce."

Whistling, he takes off, strolling up the boardwalk, eyeballing all sorts of different shops.

Leaving me to wonder, what will Ms. O'Mara's nephew try to steal next?

CHAPTER 34

Meredith flags me down outside the church, ten minutes before rehearsal the next day. I have Emma with me.

"My turn to babysit," I tell Meredith.

"I'm not a baby," says Emma. "I'm six years old. Deal with it. Hi, Meredith."

Meredith smiles. "Hi, Emma."

"What's up?" I ask her.

"All of a sudden, they want me to play Fairy."

"I'll play fairy with you, Meredith," says Emma, beaming.

"Emma?" I say. "Meredith and I are trying to have a grown-up discussion."

"Why? You're not grown-ups. You're twelve."

"Which is more grown up than you."

"Maybe. But you don't *act* more grown up than me. . . ."

I ignore her. I can tell Meredith needs to talk. "Who's this fairy they want you to play?"

"A fairy without a name. She's just, you know, Fairy."

"Well, that's great."

"Nuh-uh. Fairy has a lot of lines."

"So? You can do them. Pretend you're singing the lines. . . ."

"Ms. Sherron says that might be how we end up doing it. . . ."

"Great. Let me see the sides."

Meredith passes me the script. Her hands are trembling.

"Okay," I say. "These are just like lyrics. They even rhyme."

Meredith peers over my shoulder. "You're right. That makes it a little easier."

Meredith and I run the lines. Emma is our audience. The more Meredith recites the words, the better, more at ease, she gets.

While we're rehearsing, Schuyler ambles over. "What are you guys doing?" he asks, probably wondering if we've been talking about him and his sticky, taffy-snitching fingers.

"Shakespeare," says Emma. "He writes plays filled with fairies."

"This is my little sister Emma," I explain.

"Pleased to make your acquaintance," says Schuyler, offering her his hand and dipping into a curtsy.

"Charmed, I'm sure," says Emma, because, I

think, she's heard me say it when I'm goofing around.

"They just slammed Meredith with a bigger role," I tell Schuyler.

"But Jacky's making it easier for me to understand what I'm saying."

"It's fun," I say.

"Cool," says Schuyler. "Do what you love, and you'll never work a day in your life."

"My daddy says that," says Emma.

"Smart man. See you guys later. And, Jacky? Say hi to your sister for me."

"Olivia?"

"No. Sophia."

He strolls away. Probably off to do what he loves: stealing stuff. You do that, you never have to work a day in your life, either. Unless you wind up in prison. Then you have to make license plates or work in the laundry ironing other inmates' underpants.

CHAPTER 35

Riley swings by the church on her bike to take over the Emma watch.

"I'm ready to take over my part of the shift," says Riley. "I think I found the bathing suit I need. Come on, Emma."

Emma props her hands on her hips. She learned to be defiant around the age of two.

"You guys keep passing me around like a hot potato!" she whines.

"Because it's summer, Emma," I say. "Everything's hot."

"Hey, you want French fries?" says Riley. "Those are hot potatoes."

"Okay," says Emma, with a gleam in her eye. "French fries *and* cheese pizza."

Another thing she learned at the age of two? How much she loves cheese pizza.

Riley looks at me. I dig into my pocket. "Will two dollars help?"

"Couldn't hurt. All I have is fifty cents."

She takes my money (yes, I will spend the entire summer broke, I'm sure of it) and leads Emma off to the boardwalk.

Meredith and I head down to the church basement, ready to rehearse. Meredith is feeling confident that she can handle the speech we've been working on. There's only one problem: The Fairy's scene is with Puck. Travis Wormowitz.

"'How now, spirit!'" says Travis at the top of the scene. He strikes this pretty goofy pose. "'Whither wander you?'"

Meredith launches into her lines, adding some willowy and mysterious modern dance moves. "Over hill, over dale, / Through bush, through briar, / Over park, over pale, / Through flood, through fire.'"

She gets her lines right, but to my amazement, she puts an awesome spin on them, like she's half singing, half rapping them. With her beautiful voice, it really makes you think she's a fairy, because humans don't sound that good!

"'And I serve the Fairy Queen,'" says Meredith. "'To dew her orbs upon the green.'"

"Cut!" shouts Travis. "Excuse me, Meredith, but this isn't some kind of hip-hop show starring LL Cool J or Run-D.M.C. This is supposed to be Shakespeare—not amateur night at the Apollo Theater! Do it right or go back to Harlem where you belong!"

Every adult in the room is staring at him. Some have their mouths hanging open. Latoya Sherron has her arms crossed over her chest. She looks mad. Very, very mad.

Even I know the Apollo is a world-famous theater in the Harlem neighborhood of New York City. Tons of African-American performers got their start there, like Diana Ross, the Jackson 5, Aretha Franklin, Stevie Wonder, and Mariah Carey. Shakespeare would've been lucky to see his plays performed there!

But for Travis Wormowitz to say those horrible things to Meredith, like she's doing something wrong and doesn't deserve to be here? Well, there's only one thing for a best friend to do.

As I'm marching over to the stage and rolling up my sleeves to sock Wormowitz right in his wormhole, I see Scott, the director, looking at Ms. O'Mara. She nods. He nods back.

"Travis?" says Scott. "Let's take a walk. Outside."

"What? You have notes? For me? I only said, like, one line and I said it absolutely perfectly!"

"Outside," says Scott. *"Now."*

"Fine. Whatever." Travis stomps up the steps. He doesn't prance, skip, or fairy-hop. He stomps.

And he never, ever comes back to that church basement.

Ms. O'Mara comes over to me.

"Jacky?"

"Yeah?"

"Have you been doing your homework?"

All I can do is nod and try to remember how to breathe.

"Good. Because you're our new Puck."

"Okay," I say. "Wh-wh-who's my understudy?"

"Nobody right now. So, Jacky? Don't mess this up."

I nod again.

So, my darling daughters, as you can see, not getting the part of Puck wasn't my colossal mistake that summer because, eventually, I did.

But hang on.

Mom's big, embarrassing belly flop is still on its way.

CHAPTER 36

When you're in a play, your cast becomes your new family.

And nobody wants to be in a family with someone who is downright mean and nasty to someone else in that family. When my friends and I talked about it later, we all agreed Travis was totally disrespectful to Meredith. You can't do that and stay in the family (unless, of course, it's your biological family—otherwise, Sophia would've kicked me out of the Hart family for messing up her under-the-boardwalk romance with Schuyler).

After Travis's dramatic exit, we rehearse a few scenes with *me* as Puck. I amaze everybody (including myself) with how well I know the lines. See, mornings at the Balloon Race booth are kind of slow. I have plenty of time for memorization. I've been working the lines into my booth spiel to make sure they really stick in my brain cells.

And, ta-da! Since I actually know the lines, I don't stutter. (Even though on the inside I'm shaking like the last leaf on a tree being attacked by a leaf blower.)

"We should celebrate!" says Bill when rehearsal's over around eight o'clock. "Who wants to grab a slice?"

Everybody's hands shoot up.

Except mine.

"If it's okay with you guys, I just want to head home," I say. "It's been a long, strange day."

"Sure," says Bill. "I'll walk you."

"Maybe tomorrow," I tell him.

"Okay," says Bill, sounding disappointed.

"Don't worry, Billy Boy," says Meredith. "Jacky's still crazy about you. . . ."

I give her a double eyebrow raise and a *Whaaaat?* look. Meredith ignores both.

"She just has a lot to think about," she says.

"True," says Dan.

"Like how is she going to get Riley to cover more of her babysitting slots now that she has such a major role?" adds Jeff.

He's right. Plus, what am I going to tell Mom and Dad? I promised them my role as Mustardseed wouldn't interfere with my chores at home or my job on the boardwalk. And they're counting on me to pitch in with Emma.

So, I actually *do* have a lot to think about.

"Maybe next time?" I say to Bill.

He smiles. His hazel eyes twinkle. "Next time."

☆☆☆

It's dusk. I decide to stroll down the beach to the band shell. To see the stage where I will be playing Puck, one of Shakespeare's best parts, in front of thousands of p-p-people.

As I approach the band shell, I hear loud, angry voices shouting from the stage. They're accompanied by even angrier electric guitars that seem to know only two chords.

"We're Toxic Trash!
Come hear us thrash!
We're better than the Clash!
We'll give your ears a rash!"

CHAPTER 37

I study the two guys on the stage.

I'm pretty sure it's Bob and his friend Ringworm (I seriously need to learn his real name). They've both done something spiky with their hair. They're also dressed in ripped T-shirts and black leather pants, and have chains dangling off their belts.

The two boys are manically hopping around a boom box (that's a portable music machine the size of a suitcase), shaking their heads, pumping their fists in the air, and screaming at the empty beach. They're imitating hard-core punk rockers, which, in the late '80s and early '90s, meant bands with names like the Misfits and Gorilla Biscuits.

Remember how Bob was making my stomach flip and feel funny? He's doing it again. But it's a new kind of funny. The kind you get with stomach flu.

When the music stops, Bob thrusts his make-believe microphone up toward the sky.

"We're Toxic Trash," he announces. "And we want your vote, Seaside Heights!"

Since there's no one else in the audience, I applaud.

"You've got mine," I say. Of course I have no idea what Bob and Ringworm are running for.

"Jacky?" says Bob after he squints enough to recognize who's clapping for him.

I give him a wiggle-finger wave.

He hops off the stage.

"Aren't we awesome?" he asks.

"Well," I say with a smile, "your hair sure is."

"Thanks. We're going for the whole punk look. I might dye mine pink for the show."

"What show?"

"The Battle of the Bands! It's gonna be here on the beach."

He shows me a crinkled flyer.

"The battle takes place right here on this stage," snarls Ringworm. "Right before your stupid Shakespeare show."

"Um, our Shakespeare show isn't going to be stupid."

"Sure it is," says Ringworm. "It's Sh-Sh-Shakespeare, isn't it?"

Well, Bob may be trying to become a decent human being, but his sidekick, Ringworm, is definitely slipping back into familiar kindergarten-bully territory on me.

"We are so going to win this thing!" says Bob. "All we need now is the entry fee and a ton of hair gel."

"Hey, you got any money, Jacky Ha-Ha?" says Ringworm, giving me a mean look. "Because we need two hundred more bucks to enter the Battle of the Bands."

"No . . . I . . ."

He moves closer.

"Don't w-w-worry, Jacky. We'll pay you back wh-wh-when we w-w-win. First prize is a thousand b-b-bucks."

"I don't h-h-have any money," I say, taking a step back.

"Sure you do. You have a job. People with jobs always have money. . . ."

Unless they give most of it to their parents, I think but don't say. All I want to do is get out of there fast.

"Whoa," Bob says to Ringworm. "Ease up, bro."

"Aw, you've gone all soft, Roberto. Just because Jacky Ha-Ha smiled at you once . . ."

I'm trying to decide where exactly to kick Ringworm first and which way to run when I hear the wonderful *whoop-whoop-whoop* of a police siren and see the soft swirl of cherry-red light.

The cavalry has arrived!

CHAPTER 38

It's the Seaside Heights Police, and Dad's working the night shift.

He and his partner ease out of the patrol car, the way super-cool cops do on TV. The spotlight beam of a flashlight hits us. I feel like tap-dancing for joy.

"Jacky?" says Dad as he and his partner amble closer. "These boys friends of yours?"

"Not exactly," I mumble.

"What's the problem, Officer?" snarls Ringworm.

"We had a noise complaint," says Dad's partner, a lady I don't recognize. "Were you kids screaming and shouting about toxic trash and the Clash?"

"So what if we were? It's a free country," says

Ringworm, who, it seems, has taken over the top bully spot from Bubblebutt. Maybe they had a vote.

"It's also getting dark," says the cop. "Little kids are trying to sleep. You're keeping everybody awake. Plus, did you seriously say you were better than the Clash? Because I gotta tell you—'Rock the Casbah,' 'London Calling'. . .those are classics."

"They're old!" shouts Ringworm. "*You're* old."

"Yo, bro," mumbles Bob. "Chill."

"You two need to move along," says Dad. "Now."

"Fine!" says Ringworm. "But we'll be back for the Battle of the Bands, which, by the way, we're totally going to win, this I can tell you!"

As Ringworm and Bob saunter away, Dad flicks off his flashlight.

"You okay, Jacky?" he asks. Parents have a kind of internal radar. They know when their daughters or sons are scared. Trust me. We do.

"Yeah," I tell him. "I'm fine."

"Those two boys in your Shakespeare show?" he asks.

"No way."

"Good. They didn't strike me as Shakespeare types."

I take a deep breath. “Dad?”

“Yeah?”

“They gave me a bigger part in the show today. I might need to rehearse more. But I promise—I’ll still keep my job on the boardwalk. I’ll still bring home the exact same pay. And I can still help look after Emma.”

Dad scrunches up his face to think. “You’ll have to work harder and longer. At play practice, on the job, and at home.”

I nod. “Yes, sir. But acting in plays, being in shows—it’s what I love doing more than anything in the world.”

“Good,” he says with a soft smile. “Then at least that part won’t feel like work, will it?”

My turn to smile. “No, sir.”

“It’ll also keep you off the beach late at night, so you won’t be running into so many wannabe punk rockers,” offers his partner. “Just saying.”

“What new part did they give you in the play?” asks Dad.

“Puck.”

“Like in hockey?” says the other cop. “Do you have to skate? Is it like one of those Disney on Ice shows? Because, not for nothing, the ice is going to melt if you put it on the beach. . . ."

Dad just laughs and drapes his arm over my shoulder.

"Come on, Puck," says Dad as we walk up the beach to his police cruiser. "Let's get you home. Sounds like you have a very busy day tomorrow."

Yes, that night I rode in the backseat of a police car for the first time. To anyone who saw me, it looked like I'd just been arrested, when in fact, I'd just been rescued.

CHAPTER 39

The next day, Ms. O'Mara and I are hanging out at the church before rehearsal.

It's just the two of us. She's sipping hot tea with honey out of a cardboard cup (it soothes her vocal cords, she tells me). I'm slurping a cherry-flavored Icee. Fast. I give myself a brain freeze.

YOUCH!
The top of my skull feels like an igloo!

We both arrive half an hour early for rehearsal all

the time because that's what theater nerds do.

We're making small talk when, all of a sudden, Ms. O'Mara thanks me for making sure Schuyler has some kids close to his own age to hang out with over the summer.

I'm trying to muster up the courage to tell her about the attempted shoplifting episode at the taffy store. But I'm torn. Maybe I didn't see what I thought I saw even though I'm pretty sure I saw it. Plus, I don't want to hurt Ms. O'Mara's feelings. Then again, they might be hurt even worse if Schuyler does something stupid and ends up in jail.

But then, as if she's reading my mind, Ms. O'Mara says, "Jacky, there are some things you may not know about my nephew."

Oh, good, I think. *She knows the truth. She's going to tell me she already knows that Schuyler is a one hundred percent kleptomaniac. That he's seeing a psychiatrist and they're working on a cure for his sticky-finger-itis.*

"Schuyler's mother, my sister, died two years ago," she says.

I put down my Icee. I have a feeling this is not

the kind of story you want to slurp slushy mush through.

"His dad is still over in the Middle East," she continues. "He was one of the ones who didn't get to come home right away."

My mom, like I said, came home almost as soon as the bad guy with the bushy mustache, Saddam Hussein, was back in his Baghdad box and Operation Desert Storm was over.

"Schuyler's father is still in Kuwait—sweeping the desert for land mines and unexploded bombs. He also has to help them put out all the fires in the oil fields that the Iraqis started. It's dangerous work and it may not be finished until sometime next year."

I nod. I realize how lucky we are that Mom was a reservist who came home with the first wave of returning warriors.

"Anyway," says Ms. O'Mara, "this school year, Schuyler lived outside Philadelphia with his grandparents."

"Your mom and dad?" I ask.

Ms. O'Mara shakes her head. "His father's

folks. They're kind of old and kind of old-fashioned. They're also extremely strict. So Schuyler, being a sixteen-year-old boy who's still grieving his mother and super-angry about his soldier father not coming home with everybody else, started acting up."

"He got into trouble?"

"Big-time. The authorities were about to ship him off to a juvenile detention facility. I went to Philly and promised everybody that I would take care of Schuyler this summer. That I'd have him crew this Shakespeare show. That I'd supervise him and keep him out of trouble. So far, it's been working. . . ."

"That's great," I say, because I don't want to burst her bubble.

"So, thanks again, Jacky. You guys are helping Schuyler have the normal summer a teenage boy deserves. Especially one who's been through everything he has."

I smile nervously and don't mention that my big sister Sophia is also trying to help Schuyler have a great "teenage boy" summer, what with the romantic rendezvous under the boardwalk that I interrupted.

We finish our drinks and run a few lines.

And I don't say a word about Schuyler's taffy snatching.

If the "authorities" find out, they'll probably come cart him off to that juvenile detention facility Ms. O'Mara was talking about.

It sounds like they already have his bed picked out for him.

CHAPTER 40

After our chat, I, of course, am determined to help Ms. O'Mara do everything she can to help Schuyler. She's done a lot for me, so it's the least I can do. Plus, I really like her and I don't want to see her hurt. If her nephew ends up in kid jail, she'll be *really* hurt.

The next day, which just happens to be my day off from the balloon booth, I decide it's time to introduce Schuyler to Jersey Shore food.

"Take your pick," I say as we stroll down the boardwalk a little after noon. "Italian sausage sandwiches. Pizza. Calzones. Zeppoles."

"Lots of Italian food, huh?" says Schuyler.

"Are you kidding?" I say, doing my best Italian tough-guy accent. "Fuhgeddaboudit. Bada bing, bada boom. You want Polish instead? We've got pierogies. Greek? How about a gyro? Philly? Cheesesteaks . . ."

Yes. I did accents for each ethnic food. Except Philly. I don't know how to do that accent.

"I've got an idea," says Schuyler. "Let's eat one of everything—starting with funnel cakes!"

"Um, no thanks," I say. "Been there. Done that. Have the puke-stained T-shirt and the ruined sombrero to prove it."

"Huh?"

"Long story," I tell him.

"Okay. So let's start with a sausage and pepper sandwich."

We head to a booth where a coiled tube of sausage is sizzling next to a mound of greasy chopped peppers (green and red) and glassy onions.

"We'll take two," I tell the woman working the grill.

She scoops up some toppings with her spatula. Then she cuts up the sausage, mixes it all together, and dumps everything into two soft hoagie buns.

I pay for our sandwiches and pocket the change.

"Thanks," says Schuyler, chowing down on his hoagie. "This is fantastic."

"Definitely. Your intestines should start gurgling any second now."

"I thought you didn't have any money," says someone behind us. I turn around to see who it is.

Ringworm.

Bob isn't with him. Guess Ringworm's tired of being a wingman. He's ready to launch his solo bullying career.

"H-h-hello, Jacky Ha-Ha-Hart," he says, exactly

the same way he and Bubblebutt said it back in kindergarten. "Your daddy and his po-po friends aren't here to protect you today." He makes a *Gimme-gimme* gesture with his hand. "I saw you pocket the change. Fork it over."

"Not going to happen," says Schuyler, who, by the way, is older and bigger than Ringworm.

So all Ringworm can do is give Schuyler a dirty look. "Who the heck are you, dorkface?"

"Jacqueline Hart's theatrical colleague."

"From that stupid Shakespeare show?" sneers Ringworm.

"Indeed," says Schuyler, giving him a grand bow.

And while he's bent over, he farts. "Ah, sausage sandwiches. Such delicious gas refineries. Or, as Sir William Shakespeare once said, 'Blow, winds, and crack your cheeks!'"

I turn to Schuyler. "Shakespeare made fart jokes?"

"Totally. Aunt Kathy's teaching me his best stuff."

Ringworm goes nose to nose with Schuyler. "Well, I don't care about Shakespeare or farts. . . ."

"You should. I'm breaking some serious wind here. Now, begone from here, you roguish knave! I desire that we be better strangers."

Schuyler is seriously cracking me up.

Ringworm starts backing up. Fast.

"Thou art a boil upon mine buttocks!" Schuyler shouts after him. "Were I like thee, I would throw myself away!"

Ringworm hightails it down the boardwalk.

"Thanks," I tell Schuyler.

"No problemo," he says, shrugging his shoulders. "That guy is a real doofus."

"I owe you."

"Okay."

"Huh?"

"Invite me to your house for dinner. I'd like to say hello to your big sister. Again." He wiggles his eyebrows. I laugh.

"Okay," I say. "Come over to dinner."

"Tonight?"

"Sure. We eat at six."

"Cool. I'll be there."

"Great. I'll tell Sophia. Should I also tell her to wear a gas mask?"

"Nope," says Schuyler, patting his bloated belly. "My gas tank should be empty by then!"

CHAPTER 41

That night, Dad is working the late shift (again) and Mom is at cop school (again).

So it's up to me and my sisters to put dinner on the table.

Sophia is too busy primping to help. "Schuyler's coming? Here? For dinner? Schuyler? Here? Dinner?"

"Yes," I tell her for the five hundredth time.

"I need to fix my hair."

"You already did that!"

"But it's all wrong! It needs to be more Cindy Crawford–ish!"

She dashes off to her room to fire up her whirring blow-dryer. Again.

"We're having pizza for dinner," announces Emma, who always reverts back to Her Little Bossiness whenever Mom and Dad aren't home. "*Cheese* pizza."

"We should order two," suggests Riley. "In case Schuyler is extra hungry."

"Fine," says Emma, picking up the phone to call the pizza delivery place. "Two *cheese* pizzas."

"But what if he likes pepperoni?" asks Hannah.

"He'll deal," says Emma.

"You know," says Victoria as she sets the table, "Americans eat approximately one hundred acres of pizza every day, or three hundred and fifty slices per second. Pepperoni is America's favorite topping. . . ."

"No it's not," says Emma. "Cheese is."

"Actually," says Victoria, "cheese isn't a topping. . . ."

"It's on top of the sauce, isn't it?" says Riley.

Victoria sighs one of her *Why am I the only person in the world who understands this?* sighs.

"Hey, maybe someday I could invite Jeff Cohen home for pizza."

Victoria's eyes nearly pop out. "Jeff and I are destined to be together, Jacky. We're like Mr.

Shakespeare's Romeo and Juliet. Without the dying stuff at the end."

"You realize," I tell her, "that Jeff's two years younger than you. . . ."

"It doesn't matter," gushes Victoria. "He's so mature! And have you seen him on the boardwalk in his cow costume? He makes a very handsome heifer. Can you arrange a rendezvous?"

"What's a rendezvous?" asks Riley.

"It's French," I say. "For a meeting. Usually under the boardwalk. I'll see what I can do, sis."

Victoria hugs me just as Sophia rushes into the kitchen. Her primped and plastered supermodel hairdo makes her look like a lioness who just escaped from a wind tunnel.

"He's here!" she screeches. "He's walking up to the front door! He's going to ring the doorbell!"

The doorbell rings. I let Schuyler in.

He comes into the kitchen and says the three words that make Sophia practically swoon.

No, not *those* three words.

These: "Hi again, Sophia."

It's all it takes.

I've been under the boardwalk looking for you, but all I found was seaweed.

That wasn't me. Seaweed has green hair.

Does everybody
ave to go boy crazy
during the
summer?
YES.
Yikes!

CHAPTER 42

As I plot how to help Jeff Cohen casually bump into Victoria (in his cow costume, of course) and watch Schuyler flirt with Sophia over pizza, I wonder why I'm still thinking about Bob when, according to Meredith, I really like Bill.

It's the summer. All that sun makes everybody go a little boy- or girl-crazy. I guess that's why there are so many songs about summer lovin'. I think that's why they put Valentine's Day in the middle of the winter. There are no winter love songs. When it's February and freezing outside, you need a romantic reminder on the calendar. And cards. And chocolate. And those tiny little candy hearts that say stuff like BE MINE and LET'S KISS and LET'S NOT AND SAY WE DID.

Anyway, that night after dinner, Schuyler entertains us all with his new Sony Walkman.

A Walkman was sort of like an iPhone but without the phone part or the apps—just the music. Instead of earbuds, it came with foam-covered headphones. Plus, you needed to pop a cassette tape into its clunky case before you could hear any music. Downloads did not exist in 1991. Except on elevators.

I guess Sony called it a Walkman because it was easier to carry while you walked than a record player, something you guys have probably only ever seen at a museum or inside a hipster's house.

"This is the kind of Walkman that college professors use," Schuyler explains. "You can record stuff on it."

"Like love poetry?" says Sophia, batting her eyelashes.

"For sure," says Schuyler. "Or, you know, speeches. TV shows. Songs off the radio."

"Or poems about love," says Sophia.

"How about music?" I say this so we don't have to listen to any more mushy stuff while our stomachs are full. "Can you play music on your Walkman? Like, right *now?*"

“Sure,” says Schuyler. “But so far, I only have one cassette.”

Turns out, it’s the brand-new Paula Abdul album, *Spellbound.* Schuyler cranks up a funky tune. We all take turns slipping on the foam-covered headgear and listening to it. It has a good beat. You can really dance to it. So we do. One at a time.

When Schuyler needs to head home, Sophia walks him out the door.

And probably down to the boardwalk. I don’t tag along. I can’t handle smoochy-face yucky stuff immediately after dinner. It makes me hurl.

The next morning, over a classic cop breakfast (doughnuts with a side of doughnuts), Dad explains why he was working so late the night before.

“We’re dealing with a theft and shoplifting crime wave,” he reports.

“Where?” asks Mom.

“On the beach and the boardwalk. It’s really snowballed in the past few days. Stores are reporting all kinds of petty thefts. Tourists are having things stolen right out of their beach bags.”

“That’s horrible,” says Mom.

“Yes,” says Dad. “And if we don’t put a stop to

it soon, it could really hurt the town's tourist business."

"But, Father," says Victoria, who, as you recall, is a know-it-all, "look on the bright side. If you're the police officer who cracks the case, you'll definitely be offered a full-time job in the fall."

"Hmm," says Dad. "I guess you're right. I should go interview that angry professor again. Dig up some clues."

"What angry professor?" asks Mom.

"He's from Princeton."

"Does he know Sydney?"

"He didn't say. He just yelled at us about his missing Walkman. Someone grabbed it off his towel when he went in for a swim."

My eyes dart around the breakfast table. Nobody else is thinking it, but I sure am.

Schuyler's Walkman.

He said it was the kind college professors use.

Probably because he stole it from one!

CHAPTER 43

That afternoon, Schuyler is his usual fun and funny self.

He stops by my booth on the boardwalk.

"I'm on my way to see Sophia," he tells me. "But she doesn't get her lunch break at the restaurant for another twenty-five minutes."

I think about confronting him about the Walkman.

But Vinnie, who's in the booth behind me, has other ideas. He gives Schuyler a dirty look.

"Someone's goin' on a break?" he says. "Fuhgeddaboudit, kid. I never get one of those because my hired help here is always too busy schmoozing with the customers."

"That's not true," I say. "Not *always*."

"Well, it sure is true today, Jacky. You're so busy with your new boyfriend, you've forgotten all about drumming us up a crowd."

"He's not my boyfriend," I say, blushing a little. "He's my sister's."

Vinnie throws up both hands. "Then what's he doin' here with you?"

"He can't hang out with my sister because she's waitressing over at the Rusty Scupper and she doesn't get her lunch break for another twenty-five minutes!"

"Again with the break?"

"Sir?" says Schuyler. "Would *you* like to take a break?"

"Wouldn't everybody?" says Vinnie.

"How about I cover for you?" says Schuyler.

"You a trained carnie all of a sudden?"

"No, sir. But I won a stuffed gorilla at the Frog Bog once."

Vinnie shrugs. "Works for me. Here." He takes his money box off a shelf and hands it to Schuyler, which, I'm thinking, might be a huge mistake. "I'll be back in fifteen."

He ambles down the boardwalk. Schuyler climbs into the booth with me.

Now that we're alone, I know I should just flat-out ask him about the Walkman. But, like I said, I'm not big on confrontations. And now that I know about his mom and his dad and his trouble in Philadelphia, and how much Ms. O'Mara wants to help him, I'm not sure I want to confront Schuyler about anything. So I decide to do what I do best. Pretend nothing's wrong. Put on a happy face. Put on a show.

I turn to the crowd milling up the boardwalk.

"Step right up, gentlemen. Show your lady friends that you're a man, not a mouse. Pop a balloon and take home a gorilla the size of a house! Unless, of course, you're chicken! *Bak-bak-baaak!*"

"Don't stand too close to a bucket of KFC, buddy," Schuyler says to a guy strolling past the booth. *"Bak-bak-baaak!"*

The guy stops, glares at us.

And slaps five dollars on the counter.

He steps up to the squirt gun firing line. So do three of his buddies. Their girlfriends seemed thrilled. Guess they're all under the spell of summer love, too!

Bill is in the crowd. I see him lined up behind one of the squirt guns, waiting his turn.

"Hey, Jacky," he says, shyly giving me a small wave.

I give him a smile.

That's when Vinnie comes back, sipping a Pepsi.

"Whoa," he says. "Look at this crowd. Well done, Jacky. You and your new boyfriend done good."

When Vinnie says that, I can see Bill's heart break. Seriously, his whole body slumps like his rib cage is suddenly empty. I can read the hurt in his eyes. *First Bubblebutt and now Schuyler?* he's probably thinking. His shoulders heave as he sighs, turns, and slips away.

Shakespeare was right when he wrote "The course of true love never did run smooth."

There are all sorts of twists and turns.

And potholes.

Major-league potholes.

CHAPTER 44

I know I should run after Bill. Tell him he's got it all wrong. Schuyler isn't my boyfriend. Neither is Bob. I don't want (or need) a boyfriend. I have enough trouble just being me!

But I can't run after Bill. The crowd Schuyler and I attracted is too thick. Plus, I have yet another felonious Schuyler distraction to deal with.

Vinnie doesn't like the way his money box feels when Schuyler hands it back to him.

"Seems kind of light," says Vinnie. "I mean for a crowd this size. . . ."

"Nobody paid with coins," says Schuyler nonchalantly. "I gotta book. Sophia gets her break in five."

He takes off for the restaurant.

Vinnie counts his cash. I can tell he's suspicious.

That he thinks Schuyler pocketed a few bucks.

I realize I *have* to say something to Ms. O'Mara.

So, as soon as my shift is over, I hit the boardwalk and head for the church. Rehearsal starts in an hour. I'm hoping Ms. O'Mara will be there even earlier than usual.

I hear a strange, muffled voice behind me.

"Acky! Ate oop."

It's Jeff Cohen in his Bossy D. Cow costume. He's handing out flyers for Swirl Tip Cones. I wait up for him because I think that's what "ate oop" means when you unmuffle it.

Jeff motions (with his right hoof) for me to meet him behind the Midway Steak House (which, come to think of it, is a pretty creepy place for a cow). When we're away from the crowds, Jeff wrestles off his cow head. It takes forever.

Jeff's curly mop of hair is soaked with sweat. It's as wet as a real mop.

"Can't let the kids see me without my head on," Jeff explains. "It's against every rule in the mascot handbook."

I nod. It makes sense. Sort of.

"I just talked to Bill," Jeff continues. "He told me

that you're dating Schuyler now. Is that true?"

"I'm not dating anybody."

"What about Bubblebutt?"

"His name is Bob."

"Whatever. Bill said you were being nice to him, too."

"Because he was being nice to me."

"Oh," says Jeff. "So it's over?"

"It never started!"

"Good. Because you're breaking my dawg Bill's heart."

My turn to sigh. "It's not intentional, Jeff. I like Bill."

"Good. Because he told me to tell you that he likes you, too."

Yes, when you're in middle school, kids never talk directly to the boy or girl they like. They use go-betweens.

Which is why I have to *go between* my sister Victoria and Jeff.

"I'll talk to Bill," I say.

"Then it's all good."

"Hey, Jeff?"

"Yeah?"

"Can you bring your costume to rehearsal today?"

"Why?"

"I know someone who loves seeing you wear it."

"Is it your sister Victoria? Because I love seeing her wearing her taffy uniform. It's so white and ruffly."

"Well, she's working at the shop tonight. . . ."

"Sweet! I can make a surprise guest appearance right after rehearsal. It'll be like kismet, which means 'fate.' It's also the name of a Broadway musical. Anyway. Thanks, Jacky. I've got to bounce."

Jeff puts his cow head back on and waddles off to give away ice cream coupons.

I head to the church. Ms. O'Mara is there, helping the twins, Oliver and Quinn Reinhardt, run their lines. I grab a seat and wait for them to wrap up their rehearsal.

When they do, Oliver says, "So did you hear? Ronny got into *Miss Saigon*!"

"On Broadway," adds Quinn.

"He's leaving the show!" says Oliver.

"We need a new Tom Snout!" says Quinn.

"Any suggestions?" asks Ms. O'Mara.

I raise my hand.

"How about Schuyler?"

CHAPTER 45

This is my latest brainstorm!

If Schuyler is in the show, with a ton of stuff to memorize—like lines and blocking (that's what they call figuring out where you move during a scene)—he'll be too busy to roam around Seaside Heights on a crime spree.

"Schuyler's really good," I tell Ms. O'Mara. "In fact, he and I just improvised a whole scene at my booth on the boardwalk. Plus, he's good at insults, too. Shakespearean ones. Not, you know, the usual 'yo' mama' jokes."

Ms. O'Mara gives me a look because, yes, much like a brook, I am babbling.

"Schuyler in the show?" she says, very thoughtfully.

"Tom Snout could be a teenager," says Oliver.

"And if he's funny. . ." says Quinn.

"Oh, he is," I blurt out. "Hysterical. They should call him Schuyler Ha-Ha, except that's what they call me because my last name is Hart and I used to stutter even worse than I did at my first audition."

Now all three adult actors are staring at me.

"We'll give him a tryout," says Ms. O'Mara.

And they do.

Tom Snout is one of the "rude mechanicals" in *A Midsummer Night's Dream.* They're the comic relief—the clowns. A group of blue-collar workers in ancient Athens who put on a play to entertain the duke at his wedding. Yep, there's a play in the play. Tom Snout plays a wall dividing two young lovers, Pyramus and Thisbe.

"I play a wall?" says Schuyler when the director explains the part.

"Right. It's a joke. The two lovers have to talk through your fingers like it's a hole in the bricks."

"Cool."

"And," says Ms. O'Mara, "you'd get to wear an extremely comical rubber nose because Tom Snout should have a big snout."

I hope this works. Schuyler will look better in a funny rubber nose than a bright-orange prison jumpsuit!

"Booyah!" says Jeff Cohen, because, as you know, the guy *loves* costumes.

Schuyler plays a scene with the adult actors, including Tony Keefer, who used to star on the TV sitcom *Who's in Charge?* His face was on the cover of *TV Guide* three different times. If you ever met him, he'd tell you. At least twice.

Schuyler handles his lines in the scene perfectly. He even earns some laughs. Tony Keefer claps him on the back.

"You're good," he says. "You remind me of a young me."

I breathe a sigh of relief.

My crazy idea might actually work.

CHAPTER 46

The fake nose will be fantastic," Jeff tells Schuyler. "But I still have the costume of the summer!"

He gestures to a shopping bag stuffed with his furry black-and-white Bossy outfit.

"You must sweat like crazy inside that thing," says Schuyler.

"Not really," says Jeff, forgetting that we've all seen just how soaked he gets every time he puts it on. He could rent himself out for shampoo commercials.

We're hanging out in front of the church just as the sun sets over the ocean.

Bill, Dan, and Meredith come trooping up the steps from the basement to join us.

And it looks like Jeff had a word with Bill.

"You were good in there, Schuyler," says Bill, extending his hand to shake the hand of Schuyler, the "older" boy he thought was his rival for my affections. To tell the truth, Bill's main rival for my affections that summer was the jolly polar bear on the Icee cups. I *loved* those things. Especially the blue ones, which tasted, I don't know, blue.

"Hey, Bill," I say, "you want to come over for dinner some night?"

"Sure," he says. "When's good?"

"After the show opens, I guess. We'll have pizza. Cheese pizza."

"It's delicious," says Schuyler. "Very cheesy."

"I know," says Bill, shooting me a wink. He had dinner with me and all my sisters long before Schuyler blew into town. My pizza invitation is my subtle way of telling him not to worry. If I actually wanted a boyfriend, he'd probably be it. Why? Because he's the easiest guy to talk to that I've ever met. But remember, girls—I'd been seriously bitten by the acting bug. My one true love that summer? The theater!

Bill, Dan, and Meredith take off. They all have to be at work super-early the next day. I'm hanging back with Schuyler and Jeff because I want to keep my eye on Schuyler while simultaneously making sure that Jeff bumps into Victoria down at the Taffy Shoppe. You can stay very busy when you're trying to orchestrate young love the way Shakespeare does in his plays.

"Hey, Jeff?" says Schuyler.

"Yeah?"

"Can I try on your cow costume?"

"I don't know. Bossy represents Swirl Tip Cones. . . ."

"I won't do anything weird," Schuyler promises. "I just want to try it on for a second."

"But I'm supposed to meet Victoria later. . . ."

"You won't be late for your date."

"It's not a date," Jeff mutters as he pulls the costume out of the bag. "It's a prearranged coincidence. Here."

My guess? Jeff doesn't want to talk about his crush on Victoria in front of another guy. Boys are like that. The exact opposite of girls. We blab about everything even remotely romantic to each other every chance we get!

While Schuyler pulls on the cow suit and head, I whisper my plan to Jeff. "I told Victoria I'd be dropping by the Taffy Shoppe right after rehearsal with a special surprise."

"Does she know I'm coming with you?" Jeff asks nervously.

"No. If she did, it wouldn't be a surprise."

"Oh. Right."

"Moo meyes . . ." says a muffled voice. Schuyler. He's wearing the papier-mâché cow head, so we can't understand a word he's saying. "Ow oo I ook?"

"You look great," says Jeff, who understands

muffled Cow better than anybody, since he speaks it all day.

"Ake mah ickshure."

"I can't take your picture," says Jeff. "I don't have a camera."

(Yes, in 1991, a camera was its own thing, not an app on your phone. You also had to buy a roll of stuff called film to put into your camera. Things were positively prehistoric.)

"We need to go," says Jeff, because he's eager for his rendezvous with Victoria. "Take off the costume. I want to wear it."

"Moh-kee," says Schuyler. His hands go up to the head.

He tugs.

He twists.

He yanks.

He can't pull it off.

CHAPTER 47

Jeff checks out the back of the cow head. "You snapped the latch? Oh, man, I never snap the latch. It's rusty. . . ."

"Om orry. . . ."

"I need a screwdriver. Or a pair of pliers. Something to pry it open."

"There's a toolbox downstairs," I say.

Schuyler yanks at the headpiece.

"Don't yank!" says Jeff. "I had to give Mr. Peterson a damage deposit on that costume when he gave me the job! If you mess it up, I'll lose fifty bucks. Just stay here, Schuyler. Jacky?"

"Yeah?"

"Don't let him yank!"

Jeff runs into the church to fetch the toolbox.

Schuyler keeps trying to yank off his cow head.

"Don't yank," I tell him.

"There you are!" gushes Victoria, who comes running into the church parking lot, carrying a box of taffy. "I hoped you would be my promised surprise this evening."

I try to interrupt. "Um, Victoria . . ."

But I forgot how hard it is to interrupt a know-it-all.

"Oov ott de wong eye," says Schuyler, but of course Victoria doesn't understand him. Neither do I, actually.

"I couldn't wait for you a moment longer," she goes on. "Whenever I see you in that cow costume, I just want to jump over the moon! I brought you taffy! Some are pink and some are blue. I hope you love them as much as I love you!"

Victoria is gushing to Schuyler because she thinks the cow is Jeff! This is a mix-up of mistaken identities to rival the ones in *A Midsummer Night's Dream*!

Victoria throws her arms around the cow. Taffy tumbles everywhere.

And that's when Jeff Cohen comes out of the church with a pointy screwdriver.

Something in the way you moo attracts me like no udder lover!
I am not a happy cowboy or a jolly rancher!
CRRRAACK

"I think you're simply bovine!" Victoria gushes, her arms draped around Schuyler's neck.

He's waving his arms. Trying to shoo her away.

"Eye ot cheff!" Schuyler tries again.

Jeff sulks off into the shadows.

Chalk up another broken heart for Jacky Ha-Ha.

CHAPTER 48

I've never had a boyfriend before," Victoria tells Schuyler, who she thinks is Jeff. "I know we're not the same age, but I went to the library and did some research. Did you know that male chimpanzees prefer older females? So this is scientifically okay. . . ."

While Victoria recites some very uninteresting facts about the mating rituals of everything from black widow spiders to Wisconsin loons, Schuyler wrestles with the headpiece.

"Age doesn't matter!" Victoria declares. "I'm in love. With moo!"

And that's when Sophia joins us in the parking lot.

Why?

Because I told her Schuyler might be at rehearsal tonight, and she's super-eager to spend more time with him under the boardwalk.

Finally, the cow head pops off.

"What?" says Victoria when she sees Schuyler instead of Jeff. "I thought you were Sophia's boyfriend!"

"That's what I thought, too," Sophia says to Schuyler. "I thought we had something special. I Cindy Crawford–ed my hair for you!"

"You've got it all wrong," Schuyler protests.

"Tell me about it. I see now that you were simply using me to get closer to Victoria!"

"Who's Victoria?" asks Schuyler.

"My sister," I say, gesturing at Victoria. "You met her at dinner!"

"I thought *Sophia* was your sister."

"She is. I have six of them! Remember? Let me explain, everybody," I say.

But it's no good.

Sophia and Victoria stomp off in opposite directions.

Schuyler climbs out of the cow costume and stuffs it back into Jeff's shopping bag, which he hands to me right before he stomps away in a third direction.

Chalk up two more broken hearts on the Jacky Ha-Ha scorecard.

CHAPTER 49

I hurry home to try to explain things to my sisters.

"Sounds like you really blew it, Jacky," says Hannah when I fly through the front door. She doesn't sound as sweet as she usually does. "Victoria is in her room, reading a Jane Austen novel, hoping it will explain this romantic mess. And do you know what Sophia's doing?"

I take a wild guess. "Crying in her pillow?"

"No, Jacky," says Hannah, her cheeks flushing. "She's on the phone with Mike Guadagno! *My* boyfriend. The one who used to be *her* boyfriend! So, thanks for nothing."

Make that *three* broken sister hearts.

Sobbing, Hannah runs out of the living room and into the kitchen, where I know she keeps an emergency box of fudge stashed in the refrigerator's vegetable crisper.

"Guess she's mad at you now, too," says Riley, who's slouched on the couch and just witnessed Hannah's meltdown.

"Yeah. Tonight's been my midsummer nightmare."

Riley nods. "I heard. And you know what?"

"What?"

"I'm thinking I might need a new role model."

That's when my practically perfect oldest sister, Sydney, steps into the living room. Little Emma is right behind her, arms crossed over her chest. It's like I'm being confronted by my sibling bookends: the oldest and the youngest.

"If Jacky doesn't shape up," says Sydney, "you definitely need a new role model, Riley."

"Definitely," echoes Emma.

"I thought you were still at Princeton," I say to Sydney. "Summer school."

"I have a couple of days off this week. So I thought

I'd come home and spend them with you guys."

"She missed the pizza," adds Emma.

"And," says Sydney, "more importantly, I missed my sisters. Because family is more important than anything in this world, Jacky. Especially boys."

"Things just got a little jumbled," I try to explain. "You see, I meant for Sophia to wind up with Schuyler, and Victoria with Jeff."

"Instead," says Sydney, "they all ended up here at home. Crying."

"Hannah, too," says Riley, trying to be helpful. "She just locked herself in her room. With fudge."

"In a way," I say with a giggle, hoping Sydney will lighten up on me, "the whole thing is semi-Shakespearean. You know—summer love, mistaken identities, fudge."

Sydney does not see the humor in the situation. Not right away. Instead, she quotes her own Shakespearean verse at me. She can do that in a snap. Don't forget, she goes to an Ivy League college.

"The time is out of joint," she says. "O cursed spite, that ever you were born to set it right, Jacky."

"That's not a direct quote, is it?" I say. "I don't think any Shakespeare characters were ever named Jacky. . . ."

"It's from *Hamlet,*" Sydney tells me. "Perhaps Mr. Shakespeare's best-known tragedy. Because if you don't make things right for your sisters, and fast, that's exactly what this will turn into. A tragedy!"

CHAPTER 50

When my mom was over in Iraq, I used to write her letters all the time. I found that telling her stuff was a lot easier when I wrote it down, instead of keeping it all locked up inside me.

Now that she's home, she's so busy taking her cop class, we hardly have time to talk about anything except who's watching Emma and what to microwave for dinner and where her missing keys might be.

So, that night, I decide to write Mom a letter.

For old times' sake.

And to ask her advice.

Dear Mom:

Things aren't going so great. In fact, this is turning into the weirdest and worst summer of my young life, even though it should be one of the best. I mean, I have a big part in a big show. I have a pretty fun job. Bill still has gorgeous hazel eyes and acts like he's crazy about me.

But that's the thing. I'm twelve. I think I want to go back to being eleven, when boys were just annoying creatures who picked boogers out of their noses and ate them.

I don't like feeling all giggly and goofy around boys. Well, actually I do. And then I don't.

Have I mentioned that Bubblebutt has turned into Bob and he's not as bad as I thought he was during the first decade of my life? He needs new friends besides Ringworm, but he's actually kind of sweet.

Maybe it's Shakespeare. But, all of a sudden, I'm running around Seaside Heights thinking about love, and when I'm not thinking about love, I'm playing matchmaker for other people to fall in love. The problem is, my matchmaking is making everybody sad, when all I wanted was to help them be happy.

And then there's Schuyler. He might be a thief. Or he might just really like taffy. I know he likes Sophia, but do we, like, want her to be with a boy who might like to shoplift? Is there, like, another word besides like I could use in that sentence?

I wonder what it was about Dad that made you fall in love with him, besides, of course, him being the most handsome boy on the beach.

If you get a second, send me a reply.

You don't need to waste a stamp.

You can just slip it under my door. I'll probably be in my room. Crying.

Because I've messed up my summer and everybody else's.

Sincerely,
Your daughter JACKY

That's what I wrote. I could show it to you. It's still in the shoe box where I stashed it that night.

That's right. I never mailed that letter to my mother. Even though I didn't even need a stamp.

I figured she had enough problems without me giving her all of mine.

CHAPTER 51

The next morning, Sydney goes back to Princeton and I go back to work.

Physically, I'm behind the counter in the Balloon Race booth, but mentally, I'm trying to work out some way to set things right for Sophia, Hannah, Victoria, Jeff, and Schuyler. Shakespeare wrote a play called *All's Well That Ends Well,* and that's exactly what I need: a way to end up with everyone happy.

Because their *un*happiness is all my fault.

While I go through the motions of drumming up a crowd, my mind wanders to one of my solo speeches from the show, during the middle of all the love misunderstandings. It's about Puck putting a magic potion on the confused lovers' eyes so they'll wake up and realize who their true loves are.

I just have to find my own magic elixir.

Then it hits me.

Ice cream!

No. Frozen custard!

It's creamier, which makes it even more magically delicious than ice cream. And nothing against Jeff Cohen, Bossy D. Cow, or Swirl Tip Cones, but nobody makes better custard in Seaside Heights, New Jersey, than Kohr's. They've had their stand on the boardwalk since forever. Their specialty is orange-and-white swirl cones—where the orange custard curls through and hugs the vanilla stuff. It's very romantic, especially for a dairy product.

I'll stage an event. Offer my confused lovers a free Kohr's cone, which I'll pay for out of what little money I have left. I won't tell any of the guests who else I'm inviting. Everybody will just accidentally meet at the same time in the same place to be sprinkled with my magic potion, which I can order with sprinkles.

It could work.

But wait a second, I tell myself.

Jeff Cohen works at an ice cream shop. He won't be wowed by the offer. He can help himself to all the free samples he wants.

"No, he can't," Bill tells me when he drops by the booth after knocking off work at the T-shirt shop around three o'clock.

I just told him my goofy idea for getting everybody together and why it won't work.

"His boss, Mr. Peterson, is a real stickler about employees dipping into the ice cream tubs for freebies. He won't even let them eat the broken cones. Jeff would *love* a free orange-and-white at Kohr's."

"But how do we get everybody in the same spot at the same time?"

"We do what Shakespeare would've done," says Bill. "We send them missives. You know—those fancy, scrolled invitations sealed with wax."

Since I have to keep working, Bill volunteers to make up the invitations and deliver them to Schuyler, Jeff, Hannah, Victoria, and Sophia. I let him borrow La Bicicletta to deliver our anonymous invitations.

Nobody will know they're coming from me. Because if they did, they probably wouldn't show up.

CHAPTER 52

Bill goes to a hippie candle shop on the boardwalk and buys the cheapest sand candle they have so he can drizzle hokey-looking wax seals on his scrolled invites, which he makes out of rolled-up paper pizza plates.

Everyone is to meet at the Kohr's Frozen Custard stand at 6:30 p.m. (thirty minutes before play practice) for their free treat.

I know the guys working in the Kohr's stand, so they let me pay in advance and hide behind the counter until everybody else shows up.

If they show up.

Bill arrives first. I see him through a knothole in the wall.

I pop up.

"Get back down!" he says. "They're all coming."

Ten seconds later, I hear familiar voices.

"Victoria!" says Jeff. "Are you here for Schuyler?"

"Don't be immature, Jeff. Why would I be here for him? I'm here for you!"

"Wait, you mean you don't want to date Schuyler?" asks Sophia.

"No way," says Victoria.

"Why not?" jokes Schuyler. "What's wrong with me?"

"Nothing!" coos Sophia. Then I think I hear a smooch. It's followed by dainty clapping.

"Oh, goody," says Hannah, the one doing the applauding. "Victoria's got Jeff, and Sophia's got Schuyler, so Mike Guadagno is all mine!"

"Who's Mike Guadagno?" asks Schuyler, because he's new in town.

"A rich kid from Stonewall Prep," says Bill, helping out. "Nice guy."

"He's dreamy," says Hannah.

I take that as my cue. I pop up from my hiding place with a tray full of orange-and-white swirl cones.

"And here's your ice creamy."

Everyone groans at my rhyme, as they should.

"You're right. It's actually custard. And this is me saying I'm sorry for last night. Or, as Puck might put it: If Jacky Hart has offended, think but this, and all is mended—you did but slumber in the church parking lot, where I gave matchmaking a terrible shot. Give me your hands if we be friends. And now, Jacky Ha-Ha her paycheck spends!"

Everyone applauds when I finish my speech.

"That was the bomb, Jacky," says Schuyler, pulling a roll of cash out of his pocket. "Let me pay for this. . . ."

"No, that's okay," I say. "I already took care of it."

"I insist. Aunt Kathy just—"

He doesn't get to finish that thought.

Bubblebutt and Ringworm cruise up the boardwalk.

"We'll take that," says Ringworm. "We need more money for the Battle of the Bands entry fee."

That's right, you guys, I apologize. Come to my booth, I'll give you a prize.
Because it rhymes.

"You can be, like, our official sponsor," says Bubblebutt, trying to be nice.

Schuyler strikes a pose and points his finger toward the sky. "Begone from this place, ye fat guts!"

"Who you calling 'fat guts'?" demands Ringworm.

"You!" says Schuyler.

"Takes one to know one."

"Good sirrah, I bid you adieu!"

"Huh?" says Ringworm.

"Get outta here!" shouts Jeff, translating Schuyler's overblown words.

"I'm sorry, Jacky," says Bob.

"He called us 'fat guts'!" says Ringworm, elbowing Bob in the ribs. "Let's get him, man."

"But—"

"Don't wimp out on me, Bubblebutt."

"Yo. Who are you calling 'Bubblebutt'?"

"You, fat guts!"

"You're a fat guts!" says Bob.

"No, you are!" says Ringworm.

The two sulking bullies walk away, pushing and shoving each other. After they're gone, I don't let Schuyler even think about paying for the swirl cones.

He's already done his good deed for the day.

CHAPTER 53

After rehearsal—which is pretty short for Puck, the fairies, and Tom Snout because the director wants to focus on all the scenes with the romantic leads—I head back to the boardwalk and the Balloon Race booth.

Vinnie needs me to cover what he calls the "late-late shift." Seems he has a "hot date" with Madame Maria, the lady who tells fortunes two booths down from ours.

"She read my mind," Vinnie told me. "Asked me out right before I was going to ask her. Bada bing, bada boom. It's in the stars, Jacky. The stars."

They're heading to the mainland to catch a movie. Billy Crystal in *City Slickers*. He's also paying me double to work eight to eleven.

Schuyler has no plans for the night (Sophia is working until midnight at the Rusty Scupper). He has some time to kill and decides to kill it with me in the booth. Bill doesn't join us because his dad needs him at home.

"The toilet's gurgling. Dad can't reach the shutoff valve. Needs me to crawl behind the commode. Good times."

I wish him luck and thank him again for all his help setting things right with my sisters and their assorted suitors.

Later, I wish Bill had been with me.

We have a lot of college-age kids trying to impress their girlfriends on the boardwalk late at night. They'll keep playing until they win a prize big enough to make their dates squeal.

As you might imagine, we rake in a lot of cash on the late shift. I'm drawing the crowd, Schuyler is manning the money box.

"Is this legal?" he asks, flapping a five-dollar bill some guy just handed him. The money's been defaced with a rubber stamp that turns Abraham Lincoln into Mr. Spock from *Star Trek*.

"Vinnie will take it to the bank," I say, because

Schuyler can't remember which one of the half dozen fraternity boys lined up on the squirt gun firing range handed it to him. Plus, we're way too busy to worry about it right then and there. "If it's a problem, they'll figure it out."

That's when Jeff Cohen, in full costume, stumbles up to our booth. Both hands are on his cow head.

"Uh ee a ittle elp, acky."

I think he needs a little help. I'm getting better at deciphering his muffled cowspeak.

"It's uck. . . ."

Sounds like the head is stuck.

"Come on," I tell him. "Slip around to the back of the booth where no kids can see you. We don't want to violate that mascot code of ethics. Can you watch the booth?" I ask Schuyler.

"No problemo."

I hurry out of the booth and guide Jeff behind the back wall. I grab a pair of needle-nose pliers we keep under the counter for fixing squirt gun nozzles. Hopefully, it'll work on the cow head's rusty hook.

After a few false starts and several grunts, the head pops free.

"Thanks, Jacky. I want to go see Victoria as the real me, not a cow. Is she at the Taffy Shoppe tonight?"

"She's at home," I tell him.

Jeff sighs. "That taffy shop will always have a special place in my heart. It's where I first saw your sister in the front window. An angel. All in white. Pulling taffy. Rolling it out on a marble slab. Made me wish I didn't wear braces. . . ."

"How'd you like to have dinner with me and Victoria and all my sisters one night?" I ask him, feeling like Puck, sprinkling the world with love potions. Or love pizzas, in this case.

"For real?" says Jeff.

"Totally. We should probably wait until after the show opens, though."

"I guess," says Jeff, his shoulders sagging.

"Of course, I'll make sure Victoria comes to the opening-night performance. And the cast party!"

Jeff lights up. "You're the best, Jacky. Now I know why Bill is so crazy about you!"

That makes me smile. Jeff heads for home, happy. I head for the booth, happy. But it doesn't last long.

Because Schuyler is *gone*.

He left a note, taped to the money box: "Sorry. I had to go take care of some stuff."

I panic slightly.

Then I open the money box.

It's empty.

That's when I panic big-time!

CHAPTER 54

Of course, that's when Vinnie and Madame Maria come strolling down the boardwalk, hand in hand, after their date.

"Yo, Jacky, you gotta check out this flick, *City Slickers.* It's about cows."

"And cattle, too," says Madame Maria, whose real name is Maria Bonadonna. Maria starts telling me about Jack Palance's character, Curly, while Vinnie goes to check out the money box.

I don't hear much about Curly.

"Yo, Jacky?" says Vinnie, seeing the emptiness inside the tin box. "Where's the moola-boola?"

I swallow hard. Try to make a joke. "Gone?"

It goes over like a lead balloon.

Long story short, I lose my job. I promise Vinnie

that I'll find out who stole his cash. He promises me I better or I'll wind up in jail.

"How much was in the box, Vinnie?" asks Maria.

"On a night like this? Fuhgeddaboudit. Had to be two, three hundred clams."

That's a lot of clams.

It's after eleven. Walking home, wishing I could make everything go back to the way it was, I come upon Dad and his partner investigating the scrawl of graffiti somebody spray-painted on the rolled-down gate of the T-shirt shop where Bill works. It's a tag from an artist who labels himself Fat Guts.

I, of course, recognize Schuyler's handiwork. I mean, it has to be him. Who else goes around armed with Shakespearean insults like "fat guts"?

I find a pay phone without Dad seeing me.

I call Ms. O'Mara's house. Schuyler answers.

"Hello?"

"Where did you go?"

"Home. Aunt Kathy came by, said I had to hurry home right away."

"And you left the money box right there? In the booth?"

"No. I tucked it under the counter and hid it on the shelf behind the Garfields."

"Do you know how much trouble I'm in? The money box was empty."

"What?"

"Somebody stole all the money! Vinnie fired me. . . ."

"I'm sorry, but I had to book. Aunt Kathy needed me to come home right away."

"Why? What was so important?"

"My dad. He was able to organize a phone call from Kuwait, but he only had, like, fifteen minutes. Look, where are you? We need to talk."

"I'm on the boardwalk."

"Stay there. I'm on my way. I can explain everything."

"You better."

I hang up the phone.

I'd hear him out.

And then I'd go ahead and make the biggest mistake I ever made in my whole life.

CHAPTER 55

I meet Schuyler at the one place on the boardwalk still serving cheese fries that late at night.

"I'm sorry you lost your job," says Schuyler as I silently pump a pool of ketchup into the corner of an oil-splattered cardboard box filled with shoestring potatoes swimming in a puddle of bright-orange cheese, which should probably be spelled *cheez,* since I don't think there is anything remotely cheese-ish in the greasy glop.

CHEESE FRIES
THE MIDNIGHT SNACK NIGHTMARES ARE MADE OF

"I didn't mean to bail on you like that, Jacky," Schuyler continues. "I just had to bounce home or I would've missed talking to my dad this week. He has to wait in line to use the phone over there. . . ."

I give him a look. It's not one of my sweeter ones. If that were true, he could have gone behind the booth to tell me that he had to leave. But maybe he didn't want me to know he was leaving. . . .

"But, hey, don't worry," says Schuyler, flashing me a big smile. "Tomorrow, I'll help you figure out who stole the money. We'll look for clues and junk. We can be like the detectives on that new TV show *Law and Order.*"

"Sure," I say sarcastically. "Let's play cops. I have nothing better to do until rehearsal. Did I mention—*I lost my job?*"

"Calm down, Jacky."

Oooh. Want to make me totally uncalm? Tell me to calm down. "Everything's going to be okay," says Schuyler. "And since you are temporarily unemployed, tonight's French fries are my treat."

He digs into his pocket and pulls out a crumpled bill. He slaps it down on the counter. It's a five.

"This is no good," says the French-fry man, looking at the bill with a scowl. "It's defaced."

Yes, thanks to some joker's rubber stamp, the Abraham Lincoln on Schuyler's five-dollar bill has been turned into Mr. Spock from *Star Trek*.

That's right. Schuyler's bill looks exactly like the

messed-up fiver we collected from the frat boys at the Balloon Race booth earlier tonight.

The one we put into the money box.

The one that disappeared with all the other cash when somebody (I'm not naming names because I don't need to) ran off with the loot and made up a bogus fairy tale about a super-long-distance phone call with his father over in Kuwait.

The one that's proof Schuyler isn't just a shoplifter, he's a thief. A thief who's willing to get his friends in trouble for his crimes.

"Hang on," Schuyler tells the grumpy guy behind the counter. "I've got five singles. . . ."

"I'm sure you do," I say, pushing my box of cheese fries toward him. "You're probably loaded. There were two or three hundred clams in that money box. Not real clams. That would be gross. Enjoy your cheese fries, Mr. Moneybags. I'm not really hungry. And that's not really cheese! It's a liquid version of whatever kind of orange dust Cheetos are covered with."

"Jacky?" says Schuyler. "Wait. Don't leave." And then it hits him. "What? You think that five-dollar bill came from Vinnie's money box?"

"Well, duh. Where do you think it came from? The starship *Enterprise?*"

I walk away. Fast.

"Jacky?" Schuyler calls after me. "I can explain."

"How about you pay first, Mac?" says the man behind the counter, who, by the way, doesn't seem all that happy about working the late shift. "Then you can do all the explaining you want."

"Sure," says Schuyler. "No problem . . ."

I pick up my pace and duck down a dark alley between two closed game booths so Schuyler can't follow me. I've lived in Seaside Heights all my life. I know shortcuts.

Furious, I stomp my way home, all the while muttering one of Puck's lines from *A Midsummer Night's Dream:* "Lord, what fools these mortals be!"

And I'm the biggest fool of them all.

I was a fool to think that Schuyler was a good guy. That he could ever *become* a good guy, given his sketchy history in Philadelphia.

I was doubly foolish to let Sophia fall in love with the guy.

That was just another thing for me to set right!

And I had to do it that night.

CHAPTER 56

He's a bad guy," I tell Sophia.

"Whatever," she says with a flick of her wrist. "I like the bad ones. I thought Sean Penn was dreamy in that movie *Bad Boys.* And, of course, I loooooove Johnny Depp. He was soooo cute on *21 Jump Street.* But he's sort of bad, too. Brooding. I like brooding."

"Sophia?" I plead. "Schuyler isn't bad that way. He's a criminal. A thief!"

"Why? Because he stole my heart?"

We're in the bedroom that Sophia shares with Sydney (when she isn't at college) and Victoria.

"No," I tell her. "Because he stole money from the booth where I work."

"Really?"

"Yep."

"Rad! Now he can take me someplace nice instead of that greasy cheese-fries place on the boardwalk."

"Sophia?" I'm tugging at my hair. "Are you even listening to what I'm saying?"

That's when Victoria waltzes into the room.

"What are you two conversing about so fervently?" she says, because she always tries to find the most complicated way to say anything. She's worse than Shakespeare that way.

"Jacky says Schuyler's no good," says Sophia. "She's dissing him to the max!"

"Because he's a thief," I say, my voice filled with exasperation. "He tried to shoplift taffy, too."

Victoria gasps. "From my store?"

"Yes."

"Well, I can't say as how I blame him. We do make the best on the boardwalk. . . ."

"You guys?"

Now I'm seriously considering yanking out all of my hair. My sisters just won't listen to me. Fortunately, that's when Dad sticks his head in the door. Probably because it's after midnight and we're talking way too loud.

What's with all the noise?
Just me, Dad. Ripping my hair out of my head.
While trying to rip apart my ONE TRUE LOVE!
For this week, anyway.

"Dad?" I say. "We need to talk."

"Seriously?" he says, stifling a major-league yawn. "It's almost one o'clock in the morning, Jacky. Can't we do the whole daddy-daughter talk deal tomorrow?"

"This won't be a daddy-daughter talk, Dad," I tell him.

"Um, yes it will be," says Victoria, because, as you might recall, she knows everything about everything. "Anytime you and Father converse, it will, technically, be a daddy-daughter chat."

"Fine," I say. "But this time, it will also be a cop-informant talk, too."

Dad gets a super-serious look on his face. "Jacky? What's this all about?"

"Your crime spree. I know who did it."

"Jacky?" gasps Sophia, choking back her tears. "Please. If you believe in the power of love . . . don't!"

Now Dad arches an eyebrow. "Sophia? Is this about that Mike Guadagno boy again?"

"It better not be!" screams Hannah from the room next door.

"It's about Schuyler," I scream back.

"Oh. Okay."

"Who the heck is Schuyler?" asks Dad.

"Ms. O'Mara's nephew. He's your thief, Dad. He's the one who stole the Princeton professor's Walkman on the beach. The one who spray-painted that Fat Guts graffiti on the rolled-down gate. The one who just robbed the booth where I work and got me fired!"

"He also tried to shoplift some taffy," adds Victoria. "But it's so delicious, you can't really call that a crime, can you, Dad?"

"Yes, dear," says Dad. "I can. I'm a cop." He gives me the two-finger *Come with me* gesture.

We head into the kitchen.

It's time for the Seaside Heights Police Department to get the 411 on their bad-boy crime wave.

CHAPTER 57

We sit around the kitchen table.

Mom and Dad are both in their bathrobes, sipping coffee out of mugs even though it's one o'clock in the morning. We have only one overhead light on (because, like I said, it's one o'clock in the morning and other people in the house are trying to sleep). Suddenly, our cozy kitchen reminds me of a dimly lit, black-and-white detective movie.

"I feel like I'm in the interrogation room on a cop show," I say.

"We call it the *interview* room, dear," says Mom. Guess she learned that in cop class.

I'm actually feeling pretty pumped, because I suddenly realize something: I'll be the daughter handing Dad a collar that could guarantee he's the part-timer who wins the full-time gig with the Seaside Heights Police Department after Labor Day. And by *collar,* I don't mean I hand him the spangly one our dog, Sandfleas, sometimes wears. *Collar* is more cop lingo. It means "an arrest."

"This kid Schuyler, Ms. O'Mara's nephew, has been in all sorts of trouble with the police in Philly," I say. "He came here for the summer to clean up his act; otherwise, I'm pretty sure he was headed for the state penitentiary."

Mom and Dad both cock skeptical eyebrows.

"The penitentiary?" says Dad.

"Well, maybe juvie. Is that what they call a juvenile detention facility? A prison for kids?"

"Only in movies, dear," says Mom.

"Oh. Well, anyway, Schuyler came here, but he didn't clean up his act. I saw him trying to shoplift taffy at Victoria's shop."

"Did he steal anything?" asks Dad.

"No. He saw me watching him before he could. He put the candy back in the bin. But the other night, he was showing off a Sony Walkman that can record and play cassette tapes. Said it was the kind college professors use. The kind he probably snatched on the beach."

Dad looks at Mom. They both nod. Okay. I have their attention now.

"And that graffiti somebody spray-painted on that rolled-down security gate, where it said 'Fat Guts'? That's from a Shakespearean insult. Schuyler's big on those. He's memorized a ton."

"Anything else?" asks Dad.

"Yes. He cost me my job!"

"How?"

"By stealing the money box out of the Balloon Race booth."

"How do you know that he was the one who stole it?" Mom wonders.

"Easy. Some college kid gave us a five-dollar bill that had been defaced with a rubber stamp to turn Abraham Lincoln into Mr. Spock from *Star Trek*."

Mom grins. "Seriously?"

I nod. "Later, when he was trying to buy my silence with a jumbo order of cheese fries, Schuyler paid with the *exact same* five-dollar bill! If you guys arrest Schuyler, get him to confess, and give Vinnie back the money he stole, maybe Vinnie will give me back my job, because I know how important it is that we all work this summer and I'm s-s-so s-s-sorry I lost my job. . . ."

I start sobbing.

Dad places a gentle hand on my shoulder. "Everything's going to be okay, Jacky."

Mom puts her hand on my other shoulder.

I blink back the tears and nod, because if I tried

to say anything, the words would stumble out in a sputter.

"I'll call this in," says Dad. "Where can we find this boy Schuyler?"

"At Ms. O'Mara's apartment. She has a place over on Bay Terrace."

"Can't this wait till the morning, Mac?" Mom asks Dad.

He shakes his head. "If the boy senses that Jacky's suspicious, he might try to leave town. He might try to do something worse."

Now I can talk. "T-t-to me?"

"It's a possibility," says Dad. "One that I'm not willing to risk."

He picks up the phone.

And then the two of us head to the police station. Dad says I'll need to repeat my statement to a detective.

On the ride, he tells me I've "done good, Jacky."

About an hour later, he wasn't saying that anymore.

CHAPTER 58

Dad and I come out of the interview room after I tell a detective everything I told my parents.

When we get to the hallway, we practically bump into Schuyler. He's in handcuffs. Two cops are guiding him by his elbows.

"What'd you tell these guys?" he asks, sounding mad.

"The truth," I say.

"I didn't do anything wrong, Jacky."

"Really? What about stealing Vinnie's money?"

"Jacky?" says Dad, shaking his head. "You two don't need to be talking to each other right now."

"Or ever!" I say, because I'm madder at Schuyler than he is at me. He made me turn into a rat fink. He made me turn him in.

Schuyler shakes his head and shoots me a nasty look as they lead him into the interview room.

"You want to sit in on this, Mac?" asks a detective.

"Yes, sir." Dad turns to me. "Wait for me out front, okay?"

I nod. "Yes, sir."

I head into the small waiting room. One of the scoop-bottomed plastic seats is already taken.

By Ms. O'Mara.

And for the first time since we met all those months ago in detention hall, she isn't exactly thrilled to see me.

I don't know what to say. So I try to break the ice with a line from our show. "'Ill met by moonlight, proud Titania.'"

"There's no moonlight, Jacky," says Ms. O'Mara, even though, come on, she *is* playing Titania. "The clouds blocked it all out tonight. The same way they, apparently, blocked out your brain. What were you thinking?"

"That Schuyler needs to give my boss back his money box."

"He didn't take it."

"Oh, really? Then why did he have that Mr. Spock five-dollar bill?"

"You mean like this one?" she snaps open her pocketbook (which is what we used to call a purse) and shows me a defaced Lincoln. "Or this one?" She shows me another.

"Wh-wh-where . . ."

"At the grocery store. And the gas station. This one"—out comes a third Spock-Lincoln—"came from Latoya Sherron because I lent her five bucks last week when she wanted to go grab a coffee. These things are all over Seaside Heights. So when the police are done interrogating Schuyler, they can come after me and Latoya."

"Wh-wh-what about the W-W-Walkman?"

"Mine," says Ms. O'Mara. "I let him borrow it. That was my Paula Abdul tape."

Now that I think about it, I guess not many college professors at Princeton are all that into pop songs like "Rush Rush" or "The Promise of a New Day."

"Jacky?" says Ms. O'Mara.

"Y-y-yes?"

"Slow down. Give your mouth a chance to catch up with your brain."

I nod. Ms. O'Mara is the one who helped me conquer my stutter, back when we were doing *You're a Good Man, Charlie Brown* and I had to enter a public speaking competition. Since she's still trying to help me, I realize that she doesn't totally hate me, even though she probably should.

I'm about to ask about my last shred of evidence, the graffiti, when the dispatcher behind the desk takes a call.

"Seaside Heights Police . . . Yes, ma'am. . . . On

your wall? Red spray paint. And you saw the perpetrator? Which way did he run? . . . Okay. I'm sending out a car. . . . No, ma'am. I don't think the boy meant anything personal by it. *Fat Guts* is just what this kid tags every time he grabs a can of red spray paint."

I look at Ms. O'Mara.

Oops.

Schuyler didn't do the Shakespearean-insult graffiti, either. Unless, of course, he just slipped out of the interview room while we weren't looking so he could spray *Fat Guts* on someone else's wall.

He's not a criminal. He's just a high school kid who can't catch a break.

Especially that summer, when I made the biggest mistake of my whole, entire life.

I made the police arrest an innocent kid.

CHAPTER 59

I decide to walk home. Alone.

Dad needs to stay at the police station to see if he can "repair the damage" I've done.

"We put an innocent boy in handcuffs, Jacky," he says. "At two o'clock in the morning. We dragged him out of bed and hauled him into the station!"

Long story short, this isn't going to look particularly great on Dad's job application for a permanent gig on the force: *Experience: Writing up parking tickets and arresting the wrong children at 2 a.m.*

I reach the boardwalk and gaze up at my old friend the Ferris wheel. Somehow, life seemed a whole lot simpler last Labor Day, when all I had to do was figure out how to scale the giant wheel's girders like a circular set of monkey bars.

"Why so g-g-glum, Jacky Ha-Ha?" sneers a voice behind me.

It's Ringworm.

"There's a phone booth right over there," I tell him. "I know the number for nine-one-one. My dad's on the force this summer and—"

"Whoa," says Ringworm, holding up both his hands. "Chill, girl. Chill. I mean you no harm. Tonight's a night for celebrating."

I study his hands. They're smeared with something red and blotchy.

"Haven't you heard the news?" he says. "Toxic Trash is gonna be in the Battle of the Bands! We scored the entry fee." He pulls a thick wad of cash out of his jeans. "Check it out. That's more money than we need! We're going to be rock stars and ain't nobody ever gonna call me 'fat guts' again like your dipstick boyfriend, Schuyler."

"He's not my boyfriend," I say, annoyed that everybody seems to think I need one.

"I just happened to see him riding in the back of a police car. What'd he get busted for, huh? Graffiti? Stealing? Ha-ha, what a loser!"

I stare at him suspiciously. He seems to know an awful lot about the trouble that Schuyler was accused of.

"Come on," says Ringworm. "I'm on my way to Bob's house. Come celebrate with us. It's par-tay time." He peels a five-dollar bill off his money roll. "We can pick up some cheese fries on the way."

"Where? Everything on the boardwalk is closed. It's three o'clock in the morning!"

"Too true. So celebrate tomorrow, Jacky Ha-Ha. Buy yourself the j-j-jumbo box with extra ch-ch-cheese and think about m-m-me."

He hands me the five-dollar bill.

I take it, just to make the skeevy guy go away so I can think.

And I'm figuring you already guessed the rest. When I flip the bill over, I notice that Abraham Lincoln has been rubber-stamped into Mr. Spock. And that red, splotchy stuff on Ringworm's hands? Up close, I can tell: It's sticky red spray paint. Because Ringworm is a sloppy graffiti artist who picked up on Schuyler's "fat guts" Shakespearean insult and turned it into his signature tag to help me frame the wrong guy.

Putting the suspicion on Schuyler was Ringworm's plan all along. And I fell for it, hook, line, and sinker. I'm thinking about calling Dad and handing him another collar.

But what if I'm wrong? What if Ringworm got his five-dollar bill at the grocery store just like Ms. O'Mara did? What if his super-weird hobby is spray-painting red flames on skateboard decks in the middle of the night?

Trust me: When you've just made the biggest mistake of your whole, entire life, you're not super-eager to make the exact same one again.

I'm pretty sure Ringworm and maybe Bob are the real criminals wreaking havoc up and down the boardwalk.

But I need more proof.

And I'm going to need help getting it.

Wow. I've caught him red-handed. Literally.

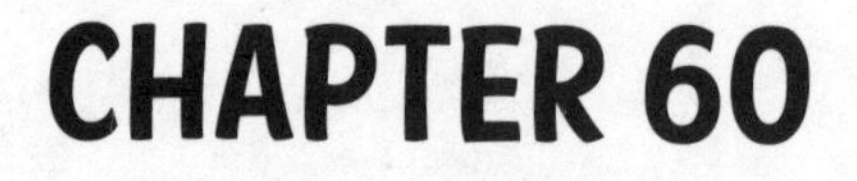

CHAPTER 60

When I wake up the next morning at around eleven—just like a normal kid on summer vacation—it hits me: I'm unemployed.

I don't have a job.

You know who else doesn't? Bubblebutt and Ringworm haven't worked anywhere since school let out. So how'd they raise all the money for their Battle of the Bands entry fee? It's pretty steep, I find out when I call the concert organizers. Five hundred bucks! I guess Bubblebutt and Ringworm made their money the old-fashioned way. They stole it.

In the light of day, the truth is even more obvious.

I bike over to Ms. O'Mara's apartment to

apologize (again) and to ask for her help.

Schuyler is there, of course, since that's where he's living this summer. He meets me on the front stoop, looking tired and frustrated.

"Hey, Jacky," he says, his face pulled way down into a mega frown. The kind you get when you ask for a pony for Christmas and all you get is a box of horse manure. "What do you want to arrest me for today?"

"Nothing. But if you want, you can lock me up for being an idiot."

"Is that a crime now? If so, how do you explain 'Ice Ice Baby' making it all the way to number one?"

"Seriously, Schuyler. I'm so sorry."

"Really?"

"Yes."

"Prove it."

"How?"

He gestures grandly toward the door. "Step in and enjoy some of my aunt's delicious pancakes."

I hesitate.

"Um, isn't Ms. O'Mara a terrible cook?" I ask.

"The worst," whispers Schuyler. "She's so bad, I usually pray after the meal. This will be cruel and unusual punishment."

I nod. "Exactly what I deserve."

We head inside. I tell Ms. O'Mara again how sorry I am. And then I prove it to Schuyler by sinking my knife and fork into a stack of the slimiest, foulest, most half-baked pancakes ever to spend time on a griddle. Schuyler empties the last drips out of the syrup bottle, so I have to eat mine raw. Which they kind of are. Raw. Once you break through the burned crusty shell, there's still soupy batter oozing out of the middle.

After I choke down a few bites and guzzle some orange juice to wash the taste of half-cooked Bisquick out of my mouth, I tell my brunch (and I use that term loosely) companions my theory.

"I think Bubblebutt and Ringworm are the ones behind all the thefts and stuff up and down the boardwalk and beach. I think they did it to raise money for their Battle of the Bands entry fee."

I give them my evidence. The paint on Ringworm's hands. The wad of cash in his pocket. The Lincoln-Spock five-dollar bill.

Then I tell them my big fear.

"It's all circumstantial evidence," I say. "My parents say that makes it harder to convict someone. It'd be way better if they'd just, you know, confess."

Ms. O'Mara puts down her fork. Pushes away her plate. She has a very thoughtful look on her face.

I mimic her moves. So does Schuyler. Hey, if she can bail on the pancakes, so can we.

"'The play's the thing / Wherein I'll catch the conscience of the king'!" says Ms. O'Mara, totally randomly.

"Um, we're talking about Bubblebutt and Ringworm," I say.

"Not Elvis Presley," says Schuyler.

"It's a line from *Hamlet,*" says Ms. O'Mara. "He adds a few details to a play that a troupe of traveling actors is going to perform for the king, so the king will react badly and confess to killing Hamlet's father."

"Does it work?" I ask.

"Yes," says Ms. O'Mara. "Just like a mousetrap!"

"So I need to do the same thing!" I say.

"No, Jacky," says Ms. O'Mara. "You need to build an even better mousetrap!"

CHAPTER 61

Jeff, Dan, Meredith, Bill, Schuyler, and I brainstorm our mousetrap ideas that afternoon at play practice, where, because we're getting closer to opening night, we're working on our makeup and costumes.

Since we're playing fairies (well, everybody except Schuyler), our face paint is extremely wild. We also have all sorts of wigs and hats and feathers and sparkles to play with.

I tell my friends the plan. Everybody is in.

We head down to the convenience store, home of my one true love, the Slurpee machine, during

WOW. It's like camouflage for the face!

a rehearsal break. While we walk, we toss around ideas about what we should do to "catch the conscience" of Bubblebutt and Ringworm.

"We could do it at the Battle of the Bands!" I suggest. "In front of a huge crowd!"

"Cool," says Jeff. "We can nail them in public!"

"Get them to confess to all their gnarly crimes!" adds Schuyler.

"Fer sure, dude," says Dan, who, since his part in *A Midsummer Night's Dream* is so tiny, has also been practicing his surfer 'tude.

"Um, Jacky?" says Bill. "What exactly are we going to do at the Battle of the Bands?"

All eyes turn to me, but I got nothing.

"Any ideas?" prompts Meredith.

"Well, uh, we could be a band."

"Slight problem," says Jeff. "None of us plays the guitar."

"Or the drums," says Dan.

"Or anything," says Meredith.

"I play the tuba," says Bill. "Some."

"Dude," says Dan, "nobody wants to hear a tuba at a rock concert."

That's when, finally, I have an idea. "We don't need instruments!"

"Uh, yes we do," says Bill. "It's a battle of *bands*. . . ."

"And we'll be a band of merry players!"

"Who don't play music?" says Jeff.

"Exactly. Come on, you guys, what's Shakespeare but old-fashioned, rhyming rap with a hip-hop beat? We can be the band of bards."

"Barts?" says Dan. "You mean like Bart Simpson?"

"No. *Bard* is an old-fashioned word for 'poet.' People called Shakespeare a bard. We'll chant a rap. Make it rhyme like crazy."

"I can scratch out a beat on a turntable," says Meredith, because she's the most musically gifted one in the group.

"I can make bass noises with my mouth," says Bill. It earns him a few stares. "I can."

He demonstrates. It is, as we used to say, the bomb.

"We could write up some fun lyrics about a group called Toxic Sludge," says Jeff, "which everybody will know is really Bubblebutt's group, Toxic Trash."

"We can have them bragging about stealing Sony Walkmans from professors!" I add. "Robbing money boxes on the boardwalk. Spraying graffiti in drippy red paint . . ."

"If we do it right," says Schuyler, "those guys will freak out! Just like Claudius does in *Hamlet*."

We all look at him.

He shrugs. "Aunt Kathy showed me the mousetrap scene in *Hamlet*. Claudius is Hamlet's uncle, who killed Hamlet's father so he could marry Hamlet's mother."

"So *Hamlet* is like a soap opera?" says Jeff.

"Sort of," says Schuyler.

"Wait a second," says Bill, sounding practical again as we enter the 7-Eleven. "Those other guys had to rob, cheat, and steal to raise the entry fee. How are we going to come up with five hundred bucks?"

"I'll give it to you!" says the man behind the counter, throwing up both his arms. "Don't shoot me. Please! I'll give you all the money in the cash register."

We all stare at him.

"Huh?" I say.

He lowers one hand to gesture at us. "You're robbers, right?"

"Um, no. We just came in for a Slurpee."

"Then what's with the disguises?"

We turn to look at our reflections in the plate-glass windows. We forgot we were in makeup and costumes.

Yep. If I saw us coming in, I'd freak out, too!

CHAPTER 62

We explain to the store clerk who we are and why we look so weird.

We also promise to give him two free tickets to the show. And then we all buy Slurpees and pose for a picture with him.

We head back to the church and tell Ms. O'Mara our idea.

"It might work," she says. "Shakespeare would be proud."

"There's only one small hitch," I say.

"What?"

"We need to come up with five hundred dollars for the Battle of the Bands entry fee."

"Without stealing it," adds Schuyler. "Because I'm not goin' back to the slammer. Ya hear me, copper? I'm not goin' back!"

We all laugh. Schuyler does a good gangster movie impression.

"Relax," says Ms. O'Mara. "Let me talk to a few people."

We finish our rehearsal. Afterward, we're all back in the dressing room, scrubbing our faces with cold cream to wipe away the makeup. Ms. O'Mara, who looks amazing in her Titania outfit, comes in with

Tony Keefer, the sitcom star, who's playing Bottom, the funniest of the rude mechanicals, not to mention the one who gets turned into a donkey.

"Boys and girls," says the jolly Tony Keefer, "Kathy told me about your diabolically clever scheme. Kindly allow me to pay for your mousetrap. I'm a millionaire! Did I mention that I was on the cover of *TV Guide* three different times?"

"Yes," says Schuyler. "Four times."

"No. It was only three."

"Maybe. But you told us about it four!"

Now Latoya Sherron comes into the dressing room. "And since I am one of the official judges for the contest, I don't think you kids will have any trouble at all winding up in the show. You just need to have an act and a name for your group."

"We've got both!" I say.

And then we free-form a few improvised verses for our musical mousetrap.

WE'RE THE TOXIC SLUDGE.
WE'LL STEAL YOUR FUDGE.
YOU WANT SOME GRAFFITI?
TRY "FAT GUTS," SWEETIE!
WE'LL STEAL MONEY RIGHT OUT OF YOUR BOOTH.
GRAB YOUR CASSETTE PLAYER, FORSOOTH!

CHAPTER 63

We keep rehearsing our Battle of the Bands number at every *Midsummer Night's Dream* rehearsal.

We have only a week to work out our routine, complete with break-dance moves.

Break dancing, by the way, was a very acrobatic style of dancing where you did all sorts of crazy moves and stunts and usually ended up breaking something. An arm, a leg, a wrist.

Jeff Cohen and I work on the lyrics for our Toxic Sludge number. Meredith finds some backing samples to scratch out on a turntable. Bill turns his mouth into a beatbox.

Hey, you guys! When we're done dancing, we can go try out for the
OLYMPIC GYMNASTICS TEAM!
BARCELONA 1992, HERE WE COME!

Fortunately, our scenes for the Shakespeare show are all in pretty good shape. We open ten days after the Battle of the Bands—on the same stage.

When our "Toxic Sludge" parody rap is also in good shape, I get ambitious. On the night of the big Battle of the Bands show, I arrange for Sophia and Victoria to accidentally (on purpose) show up backstage to wish Schuyler and Jeff luck.

"I'm sorry Jacky said all those mean and horrible things about you," Sophia tells Schuyler.

"Me too," says Schuyler, who's dressed all in black

leather like a punk rocker. "But she and I are cool now."

"What about us?" asks Sophia, batting her eyelashes.

"We're super-cool."

"Good. Then, since we're officially dating . . . "

Schuyler looks a little nervous when Sophia says that. Boys usually do.

" . . . I have to be honest with you, Schuyler. I don't like what you've done with your hair. That spiky Mohawk with the blue tips? I hate it. Sorry. I do."

Schuyler laughs. "It's part of the costume. For the show tonight."

"Oh. Right. You're in showbiz. Like Jacky. Well, we can work on that. . . ."

They drift off, so I go make sure Victoria and Jeff are doing okay, too.

"You're not dressing up as a cow for this evening's performance?" Victoria says when she sees Jeff in his hip-hop costume.

"No. Tonight, I'm DJ Jazzy Jeffrey."

"Oh. It's a whole new role?"

"Yep."

"My. You are extremely versatile and talented."

“That I am!” says Jeff, wiggling his eyebrows.

And then, gag me with a spoon, he and Victoria kiss. I’m serious.

“Jacky Hart?” calls out a guy wearing a headset and carrying a clipboard. I figure he’s the stage manager for the Battle of the Bands.

“Yes, sir?” I say, grateful to have something to look at besides Victoria and Jeff’s smooch-fest. By the way, I could totally tell that Victoria had been studying how-to-kiss manuals to prepare for her big moment with Jeff.

All the couples are back together. It's like Shakespeare said, "All's well that ends well." Actually, he didn't say it. He just used it as a title for a play.

"You're up next," says the stage manager, ticking a list on his clipboard. "This is your five-minute warning."

I grin because the stage manager should really be warning Ringworm and Bubblebutt.

We're about to spring our mousetrap on 'em!

CHAPTER 64

We assemble in the wings and wait for the Bruce Springsteen tribute group to finish their set. They call themselves the D Street Band instead of the E Street Band. They probably should get a D for destroying the Boss's big hit "Born to Run."

Bubblebutt and Ringworm see us waiting in the wings.

Bubblebutt looks semi-shy, with his head hanging down. I get the feeling there's been a switch in their rankings. Bob, or Bubblebutt, used to call the shots. Now it seems that Ringworm has been bullying *him* this summer. The bully has become the bullied.

"What are you doing here, Jacky Ha-Ha?" sneers Ringworm. "Why are you dressed up like that?"

"You mean like you?" says Schuyler.

"How come you're not in jail, Skee-Ball? Everybody knows you're the one who spray-painted all that Fat Guts graffiti up and down the boardwalk."

"You mean," I say, "that's what you wanted everybody to think when you did it, right?"

"Ha! I didn't do nothing."

"Which means you did something."

"Huh?"

"They call it grammar. Study it sometime!"

The D Street Band strum their final chord and take a bow. Their friends and family applaud politely. Bob is looking at me like he wishes he could say he's sorry. But he doesn't.

"And now, ladies and gentlemen," booms the announcer through the mammoth speakers ringing the stage, "please welcome our next group, representing Shakespeare Down the Shore, here they are, one of Latoya Sherron's personal faves—the Band of Bards!"

WE ARE THE THIEVES
FROM TOXIC SLUDGE. WE'D BE
IN JAIL IF WE MET A JUDGE. WE
ON THE BEACH ROBBED ANY MONE
WE SPRAYED GRAFFITI

TOLE A WALKMAN
3OX WE COULD REACH.
LAUGHED OFF OUR BUBBLE BUTTS.
DID IT UP IN RED, YO,
WE'RE "YE FAT GUTS!"

The audience goes crazy. (Don't forget, I have a HUGE family.) I give Ringworm a wink.

"Pay close attention to the lyrics," I tell him. "I think you'll enjoy them."

"Not as much as you are going to enjoy ours!" shouts Ringworm. "You're just like Schuyler. You're a thief, Jacky Ha-Ha!"

At that second, I didn't know what he was talking about. I couldn't worry about it either. We were on!

We rush onstage and strike our opening break-dance poses. Meredith scratches out a riff on the turntable. Bill lays down a steady beat into a microphone pushed tight to his lips. We launch into our rap about Toxic Sludge—a punk band of roving criminals terrorizing Seaside Heights.

Everybody watching the show is cracking up.

Except, of course, the members of Toxic Trash waiting in the wings. Ringworm is seething. If life were a cartoon, there'd be steam shooting out of his ears. Bob, on the other hand, is looking embarrassed. Like he wishes Ringworm weren't his friend. Like he wishes he could just disappear.

We repeat the line with Bob's nickname in it.

"We sprayed graffiti, laughed off our bubble butts. Did it up in red, yo! We're ye Fat Guts!"

"And though this might just make you squirm," ad-libs Schuyler. "My first mate is called Ringworm!"

I can't blame Schuyler. After all, Bubblebutt and Ringworm totally tried to trash his good name and make everybody think he was the one doing all the illegal stuff. It's only fair that he gets to return the favor.

I glance off into the wings.

Ringworm (I really do need to learn his name someday) is furious—and not just because we've worked him into our rap and told Seaside Heights what he's been doing on his summer vacation. He's mad because Bob is leaving!

He's taking off his studded leather gloves, combing out his Mohawk, and heading home.

Huzzah! Our mousetrap worked!

As we prance offstage triumphantly, Ringworm is smiling.

"Did you enjoy that?" asks Schuyler.

"Yeah," says Ringworm. "That was super-cute.

You looked like a bunch of ballerinas out there. But you know what, Sky-dork? You're going to enjoy our song even better."

"What?" I say with a laugh. "You're doing a solo act? Looks like your partner in crime abandoned you."

"You mean Bubblebutt?" sneers Ringworm. "No problemo. I've got an understudy for that big chicken."

And guess who steps out of the shadows, dressed up in the same kind of heavy metal costume as Ringworm?

Travis Wormowitz.

CHAPTER 65

I think you nerds know my big brother, the high school theatrical superstar Travis Wormowitz," says Ringworm.

"The one you jerks got kicked out of the Shakespeare show," adds Travis, giving Meredith a really dirty look. "Not that I'm bitter. No. I'm furious! You wimps cheated me out of my first major Shakespearean role."

"Travis is your b-brother?" stammers Bill.

"Duh," says Ringworm. "How do you think I got my nickname? I'm Reggie Wormowitz. Bob turned it into Ringworm. So I turned him into Bubblebutt. Because he has one. That thing jiggles, man."

"Excuse us, children," says Travis. "We're on!"

"And when we do our number," gloats Ringworm (I mean Reggie Wormowitz), "everybody will know who the true thief in this town is! Schuyler!"

The Wormowitz brothers do a chest bump. Their Mohawks shimmy when they collide.

To spare you the pain of hearing about Toxic Trash's head-banging heavy metal screed, which had only two guitar chords in it, I'll make a long story short. The Wormowitz brothers do a loud and annoying song about "Schuyler, the liar, the thieving highflier, the sneaky crooked smiler." They even have a verse about Schuyler being arrested and sent to prison, which isn't totally true. But the audience doesn't know that.

That's right. They had the same plan that we did, but worse—using the Battle of the Bands to trash Schuyler's reputation in front of all of Seaside Heights even before they knew we'd be at the Battle of the Bands singing about *them*.

We're standing in the wings, watching the nasty brothers publicly humiliate Schuyler.

"He's a dog, that Schuyler. A nasty ol' rottweiler!" Travis snarls into the microphone while Reggie thrashes out the other chord he knows on his electric guitar.

"Guess they had the same rhyming dictionary we did," says Bill.

"Our lyrics were better, man," mutters Jeff.

"Our music was better, too," adds Meredith.

"Um, you guys?" I say. "We didn't enter the Battle of the Bands to win the competition. We did it to clear Schuyler's name by having Ringworm confess to all the crimes!"

"Gee, Jacky," says Schuyler sarcastically. "That sure worked out well, didn't it?"

It's true. My mousetrap plan flopped. We wasted all that time working on our rap and our breakdance moves. We have nothing to show for it except some goofy costumes and even goofier hair.

Plus, now all of Seaside Heights thinks Schuyler's a thief and a liar.

And it's all my fault.

CHAPTER 66

Schuyler glumly turns off his Walkman, the one Ms. O'Mara let him borrow. There's a blank cassette inside where the Paula Abdul tape used to be because Schuyler wanted to record our rap and then Bob's confession.

So much for that foolproof plan. I'm surprised anyone can look me in the eye right now.

But seeing the Walkman, I suddenly have a new idea!

"This isn't over!" I say.

"You're right," says Schuyler. "Sounds like they've got a third verse. . . ."

The Wormowitz brothers continue to thrash their guitars and stomp all over Schuyler's reputation.

"Pretend like you don't know me," I tell everybody.

"Easy," says Schuyler. "Because I sure wish I didn't."

I ignore that. I have too much to do and not much time to do it.

First, I run around the backstage area, hastily putting together a new costume by borrowing stuff from the other acts and raiding the trunk we dragged over from the dressing room. I wind up with a curly blond wig, a floppy hat, a fuzzy boa, and some very dark bug-eye sunglasses.

Next, I ask Schuyler if I can borrow his Walkman. "I want to record something."

"What do you want to record? All those horrible things Toxic Trash are saying about me because you used to believe it, too?"

"Look," I tell him. "I'm sorry. Getting you arrested was the biggest mistake I've ever made in my life and, hopefully, I've learned my lesson. In fact, I've definitely learned my lesson. But this is no time for whining. 'Up, and away! / Our soldiers stand full fairly for the day'!"

"Huh?" Schuyler puzzles.

I grab the Walkman out of his hands.

"It's Shakespeare. What? Do you think you're the only one who can memorize obscure quotes? Disappear, you guys. It's time for Jacky Ha-Ha to get into character."

"Who are you going to be this time?" asks Dan.

I smile and put on my best Valley girl voice. You know, like, all my sentences end with a question mark? Even when they're not questions?

"I'm, like, Toxic Trash's number one fan? Seriously, dudes. I am!"

Toxic Trash finish their horrible song. Maybe one person in the whole crowd claps, but that might just be the sound of a pizza box being thrown in a trash can.

"Scram, you guys," I tell everybody. They scurry away.

The Wormowitz brothers waltz offstage, slapping each other high fives.

"We were so totally awesome!" says Reggie.

"I am always awesome," says Travis, looking around the backstage area, seeing nobody he recognizes from the play (which means my costume is working!). "Guess those middle school dorks couldn't stand the heat. They all ran home to their mommies. Except Schuyler. He ran home to his horrible aunt. The one who cut me from my first professional Shakespeare gig!"

"We showed them!" says Reggie, who will always be Ringworm to me, because just thinking about him gives me a rash.

I take in a deep breath. It's time for the performance of my life. First, I have to pretend that I loved the Toxic Trash show. And, more important, I have to do it without Travis figuring out who I am!

CHAPTER 67

"Wow!" I gush as I press the record button on Ms. O'Mara's professor-style Walkman. "I'm Brianna, from Long Beach Island, and I am in loooove with your music! You guys, like, rock!"

Like, omigod! You two are très radilicious! And your music? It's grody to the max!
Um, thanks. I think.

Ringworm does a double heavy metal thumb-and-pinkie wave at me. "Chya! Totally!"

"Thanks," says Travis. "Usually, I perform in nonmusical shows. But I was glad I was able to demonstrate my range as a performer. I'm quite good, aren't I?"

"The best!" I say, happy that he doesn't recognize me.

I'm also trying to imitate the way Sophia is around boys. The way the young romantic leads in *A Midsummer Night's Dream* behave when they are under the love potion's potent spell. In other words, I act super-goofy.

"You looked so mean and nasty out there!" I say in my Brianna Airhead voice. "I like the bad ones. I thought Sean Penn was dreamy in that movie *Bad Boys.*"

Yes, now instead of quoting Shakespeare, I'm quoting my big sister Sophia.

"And, of course, I loooooove Johnny Depp. He was soooo cute on *21 Jump Street.* But he's sort of bad, too. Brooding. I like brooding."

Ringworm sneers. "You want bad? I'll give you bad."

"Please," I say, batting my eyes. I got that move from Sophia, too. "Tell me everything. And is it okay if I record you? Because, well, I'd totally like to fall asleep every night with your voices in my headphones."

"No problemo," says Ringworm, puffing up his chest. "Me and my lame ex-friend, Bob? We tore up Seaside Heights this summer."

"I bet if the world knew that," I say, fawning over him, "they'd never call you Ringworm again."

"They better not! My name is Reggie. Reggie Wormowitz."

I hold up the Walkman.

"Could you repeat that? I want to remember it, always."

"I'm Reggie Wormowitz!" he shouts into the tiny microphone on the edge of the cassette recorder.

"And I'm his big brother, Travis. The guy who should be starring as Puck in Shakespeare Down the Shore this summer. But the casting system was rigged. Sad."

"Bob and me robbed, like, a half dozen game booths, man," boasts Reggie. "Stole all the cash out of this one balloon-pop stand where that clown

Schuyler was supposed to be standing guard. Totally framed him."

"Which was doubly sweet," adds Travis, "because this chick who stole my part in *A Midsummer Night's Dream* worked there until they got her fired."

The Wormowitz brothers slap each other five. Inside I'm fuming, but outside I clasp my hands and bat my eyelashes like I'm impressed.

"I stole an awesome Walkman, sort of like yours, out of this one dorky dude's beach bag," brags Ringworm. "Bag had an orange, tiger-striped *P* on it."

"That's for 'Princeton,'" I say. Then I catch myself. Brianna Airhead would not know that. "Or it could be for, you know, tiger pee?"

"Huh," says Ringworm. "Probably. I did graffiti, too. Because I didn't like that dude Schuyler calling me 'fat guts.' I have a glandular issue."

"So you made it look like he did it?" I gush. "That is *so* clever."

"Yeah, he even got arrested for it! And then, to seal the deal, Travis and me wrote that song you just heard about him."

"Will that be on your first album?"

"Totally!"

They tell me everything.

Which means they're also telling the Walkman everything. I have their full and complete confessions on tape. And since they gave me permission to record it, I think that makes it admissible as evidence.

Yeah. The Harts watch a lot of cop shows on TV.

CHAPTER 68

Early the next morning, I tail Dad and his Seaside Heights PD patrol car on my bike.

Why don't I just immediately hand over my tape-recorded confessions? Well, I'm a little like the girl who cried wolf. My "evidence" misled Dad once. It'll be better, I figure, if he discovers the tape on his own.

Dad and his partner don't see me pumping La Bicicletta behind them, because Dad isn't the one driving and checking the rearview mirror. His partner doesn't know who I am. When they stop at Dunkin' Donuts to get coffee (and probably doughnuts, since, you know, they're cops), I use my boardwalk ringtoss skills to throw the cassette tape with the Wormowitz brothers' confession through a partially open window.

BAM!
PERFECT SHOT!!
SEASIDE HEIGHTS PD
We have a winner!
We also have two losers: Reggie and Travis Wormowitz!

It lands on Dad's seat.

I want him to be the one to discover the evidence that'll bring the summertime crime spree to a stop.

It might help him land the full-time gig after Labor Day.

It might also help him forget (or at least forgive) my jumbo-sized mistake. I know I sure learned my lesson—a lesson best summed up by another line from Shakespeare. It's true. The guy has the right words for any situation. This quote, which I have tried to engrave on my heart, comes from that play *All's Well That Ends Well.* When I read the line, I had the biggest aha moment of my summer. No, my life!

Love all, trust a few,
Do wrong to none.

CHAPTER 69

Nine days later, the Shakespeare Down the Shore production of *A Midsummer Night's Dream* has its opening performance at the same outdoor amphitheater where they held the Battle of the Bands.

Which means it's my professional stage debut. I've performed a thousand times since then, but the memory of acting in front of a huge crowd on a summer night by the ocean is something I'll never forget.

The show is fantastic! Better than I imagined it could be. I don't stutter or miss a line. I also earn a few laughs, which, as you know, is my favorite thing to earn in the whole world. Laughter is always better than money. Seriously, it is!

I'm also onstage with my friends and the teacher who, more than once, has, more or less, saved my life—or at least helped guide it in the right direction. Ms. O'Mara is terrific as Titania.

In this same interlude it doth befall that I, one Snout by name, present a wall!

And my new friend, Schuyler? He makes an awesome Tom Snout *and* Wall!

Being on that stage with a cast of *professional* actors made me realize that if I could perform for a living—if I could become a professional, too—I would never have to work a day in my life. Of course, that was something Mom and Dad had already tried to explain to me when they shared their early-summer daydreams about becoming cops. Just like Dorothy in *The Wizard of Oz,* I guess I had to learn it for myself, huh?

When I say my last line, which is also the very last line in the play, in my mind, I'm saying it directly to Schuyler. I'm apologizing one last time for falsely accusing him of committing someone else's crimes.

When we take our curtain call, Schuyler stands right next to me and clasps my hand.

We be friends. We restore amends.

EPILOGUE

After the show, I'm a little late to the opening-night cast party.

I need to celebrate with my family first.

For cracking the big case, thanks to an anonymous tip he received in the form of a cassette tape he discovered on the passenger-side seat of his cop car, Dad has already been offered a permanent job on the Seaside Heights police force.

No, he didn't recognize my voice as the interviewer on the tape. Even at age twelve, I was pretty good at putting on voices. And when I pretended to be that gushy and goofy about two boys, it definitely didn't sound like me. It was a character I created: Bad-Boy Fangirl.

Maybe you've seen her on *Saturday Night Live.* I still call her Brianna Airhead.

Yes, girls, that was the summer a lot of dreams came true—and not just for me. Your grandfather landed his first official cop job. Your grandmother graduated first in her class from cop school. Vinnie got most of his money back. I got my job back, and it was excellent practice for my future career in show-biz. To show there were no hard feelings, Vinnie and Maria treated me to two tickets to see *City Slickers.* I, of course, asked Bill Phillips to go with me because I could talk to him about it afterward. Remember that. If you want to talk to a boy about everything and anything, then he's probably a keeper.

It was also the summer when I quit calling Bob Brownkowski "Bubblebutt." Because he kept trying to become the very decent human being he is today. He walked out on Ringworm and changed his ways for the better.

The summer of 1991 was also famous for your aunt Victoria meeting your uncle Jeff. Not to mention your aunt Sophia meeting your uncle Schuyler, who, as you know, needs us all to keep praying for him. He's overseas, wearing a similar uniform to the one his father wore in the First Gulf War. Making his father, and all of us, proud.

Being here in London has made me remember so much about my first Shakespearean summer. The huge mistake I made and then everything I did to try and fix it.

In closing, I want to leave you with words better than any I could ever write. The ones Mr. Shakespeare wrote. The ones I repeat to myself on a daily basis. The ones I had framed in a portable little picture frame so I can take this simple reminder into every dressing room I use, no matter where in the world my talent takes me:

Love all, trust a few,
Do wrong to none.

If you can do that, my darling Grace and Tina, trust me: You'll be howling at the moon with joy on a regular basis.

AAAAAAAA-OOOOOOOOO!!!

JAMES PATTERSON received the Literarian Award for Outstanding Service to the American Literary Community from the National Book Foundation. He holds the Guinness World Record for the most #1 *New York Times* bestsellers, including *Middle School*, *I Funny*, and *Jacky Ha-Ha*, and his books have sold more than 350 million copies worldwide. A tireless champion of the power of books and reading, Patterson created a children's book imprint, JIMMY Patterson, whose mission is simple: "We want every kid who finishes a JIMMY Book to say, 'PLEASE GIVE ME ANOTHER BOOK.'" He has donated more than one million books to students and soldiers and funds over four hundred Teacher Education Scholarships at twenty-four colleges and universities. He has also donated millions of dollars to independent bookstores and school libraries. Patterson invests proceeds from the sales of JIMMY Patterson Books in pro-reading initiatives.

CHRIS GRABENSTEIN is a *New York Times* bestselling author who has collaborated with James Patterson on the I Funny, Treasure Hunters, and House of Robots series, as well as *Jacky Ha-Ha*, *Word of Mouse*, *Pottymouth and Stupid*, *Laugh Out Loud*, and *Daniel X: Armageddon*. He lives in New York City.

KERASCOËT is the pen name of Marie Pommepuy and Sébastien Cosset, a couple of French graphic novel authors and illustrators living and working in Paris.